This is going to be one hell of a ride...

It all seemed too real. Mariska was at an island resort with a hot guy who desired her. She should pounce on him, but she needed a little time to pull herself together.

"How about we take a quick swim to work out the kinks?" Jackson smiled at her, and her pulse quickened. After what she'd seen during the massage, she couldn't wait for another chance to see him sans clothes. The man's body begged to be touched, and she planned to do that a lot.

She reached into her bag and scooped out one of the four bikinis she'd thrown in. This one was red with tiny bows on each side. It was one of her favorites. "Five minutes. I'll meet you out on the beach." She heard him chuckle as she shut the bathroom door.

Mariska stared at herself in the mirror.

Live in the moment.

She'd seen the phrase on a fortune cookie a month ago. It was the saying that had inspired this trip. Tired of living in the past and worrying about what everyone else thought of her, she'd decided it was time for a real vacation. One where she could be whoever she wanted, and maybe she'd find herself.

"You better watch out, Jackson. I'm a bold woman who won't shy away from life anymore. I'm going to have my way with you...every which way I can."

Blaze

Dear Reader,

I'm so excited to be one of the newest "Blaze Babes" and I hope you enjoy this, my first Harlequin Blaze title.

Have you ever done something impulsive or crazy that turned out to be the best thing that ever happened to you? That's how my heroine Mariska Stonegate finds herself involved with an intriguing and mysterious man. She decides to give in to her instincts and finds a way to spend some quality time with a hunky stranger.

My hero Jackson Walker is a CIA agent on the run. Something has happened and now everyone is after him, and he doesn't know why. He's a good guy who has to make some difficult choices in order to survive. When he accidentally bumps into Mariska, he can't help but wonder what it would be like to have a life with this sexy woman. When she wants to spend a weekend making passionate love, he can't say no to her.

Please e-mail me at candacehavensbooks@gmail.com and tell me what you think about the book, or you can find me on twitter.com/candacehavens as well as MySpace, Facebook and LiveJournal, all of which can be linked to from www.candacehavens.com. I look forward to hearing from you.

Enjoy!

Candy

Candace Havens

TAKE ME IF YOU DARE

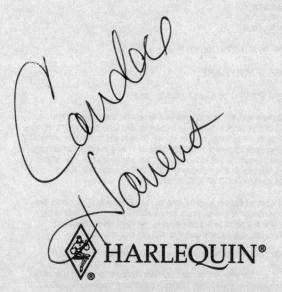

HARLEQUIN®

TORONTO • NEW YORK • LONDON
AMSTERDAM • PARIS • SYDNEY • HAMBURG
STOCKHOLM • ATHENS • TOKYO • MILAN • MADRID
PRAGUE • WARSAW • BUDAPEST • AUCKLAND

Recycling programs
for this product may
not exist in your area.

ISBN-13: 978-0-373-79527-7

TAKE ME IF YOU DARE

www.eHarlequin.com

Printed in U.S.A.

ABOUT THE AUTHOR

Award-winning author and columnist Candace "Candy" Havens lives in Texas with her mostly understanding husband, two children and two dogs, Scoobie and Gizmo. Candy is a nationally syndicated entertainment columnist for FYI Television. She has interviewed just about everyone in Hollywood from George Clooney and Orlando Bloom to Nicole Kidman and Kate Beckinsale. You can hear Candy weekly on The Big 96.3 in the Dallas–Fort Worth Area. Her popular online writer's workshop has more than thirteen hundred students and provides free classes to professional and aspiring writers.

To my editor Kathryn Lye for the encouragement,
and tough love when necessary. You are the best.

Prologue

JACKSON WAS ALIVE. At least that much he could determine from the excruciating pain in his ribs every time he tried to breathe. Testing his arms and legs. He was relieved when he could move them.

Well, there's that.

As the fuzziness cleared from his brain, he remembered exactly when everything went to hell. The moment he walked into Vladimir's office at Club Loi in Rayong he had known his cover was blown. The gunrunner greeted him without his smarmy smile, a sign that all was not well. Vlad hadn't said a word, only motioned to his men.

Jackson fought, but he was one unarmed man against eight with assault weapons. Still he'd been able to take down three of them before someone had coldcocked him from the left with the butt of an XM8. That was the last thing he remembered.

His fingers found the large egg-shaped bump on his temple and he winced. *Hope I at least threw a punch as I went down.*

Forcing his eyes open, Jackson tried to survey the

room. It took a minute to focus. Paint peeled off the ceiling and the room smelled of dirty socks. He wasn't at the Ritz.

Moving slowly, he sat up on the edge of the bed. From the stiffness and bruising it seemed like every part of his body had been pummeled. Jackson pushed the pain aside. He forced himself to move. Stumbling to the dirty window, he opened it and was assailed by the smell of dead fish. Bits and pieces of a conversation between two fighting fishermen, and a flashing neon light announcing nude girls, told him all he needed to know.

"How the hell did I get to Bangkok?" The words came out in a harsh whisper. Turning toward the sink, he stared at himself in the mirror. His cheek was swollen, lip busted, but he'd looked worse. The bloodied clothes would be a problem. Rolling his neck to loosen the tension, he glanced around the room for something he could use.

He noticed a pile of folded clothes on a chair next to the door. That wasn't what made him pause. It was the typewritten paper on top that captured his attention.

You've been compromised.

If I were you, I'd run.

"Hell." Jackson shoved a hand through his hair. "A damn burn notice." He wasn't dead yet, but he would be in a matter of hours. The Company didn't like loose ends and that was exactly what he'd become.

1

MARISKA STONEGATE WAITED in the tropical paradise known as the Aqua Bar at the Four Seasons Hotel in Bangkok. The tranquil setting was in crazy contrast to the anticipation that zinged through her body.

Less than three hours ago she'd received a case file on a missing man. Desmond Gladstone, a husband and father of a toddler, had traveled to Bangkok on business three days ago. His wife hadn't heard from him since the day after he landed. At the wife's insistence, the hotel finally checked the room. Except for his bag of clothes and toiletries it was empty. The maid said no one had slept in the bed since the guest had checked in. That's when the wife panicked.

The Thai police weren't as helpful as Mrs. Gladstone would have liked. Since there was no sign of distress in his room, they believed he had wanted to disappear, or that he was having an affair. Mariska's company, Stonegate Investigative Agency, had been hired by the man's wife to find out what happened.

The case had not been a part of Mariska's vacation plans. She'd landed in Bangkok earlier in the day ready to shop for a few days, and then she would head to Phuket Beach for a long vacation.

That's what I get for turning on my phone.

Unfortunately, she had hit the on button, and now she had a case to solve before she could run away to the place of sun-kissed skin and mai tais.

It had been a tough year, and she craved time away from home, and the well-meaning friends who were constantly in her business. Her life wasn't going according to plan, not that she really had one. But she was fairly certain she hadn't spent all those years in school to work in a job where she felt like she was barely keeping her head above water.

She couldn't even go on vacation without work interfering.

Closing her eyes, she pushed the negative thoughts from her brain.

This case is a minor bump on my road to fun.

At least the gang at SIA had hired a local private detective in Bangkok to get some of the legwork done before she arrived.

Mr. Thomas had discovered Gladstone cleared customs, checked into the hotel and then disappeared. That was a start at least. The one thing that bugged her about the mistress theory was if he was in the middle of a tryst—why not stay at the Four Seasons? Room service, six-hundred-thread-count sheets, it was hard to pass up.

A call to his workplace had revealed Mr. Gladstone was on a two-week vacation and they didn't expect him back until the end of the month. Mr. G had lied to his wife.

In Mariska's handbook that made him the winner of the Most Likely to be a Scumbag award.

Soft classical guitar music played and there was a hint of jasmine in the air. She'd never been in such a relaxing bar, and wished that her surroundings would help calm her anxiety about the case. Sipping her San Pellegrino and lime, she turned on her bar stool so she had a better view of the entry.

That's when she saw Matt Damon in a beige linen suit perfectly tailored to his body. Mariska touched her chin to keep her jaw from dropping. He commanded the room as he stepped in.

Oh, my God. No way.

Unable to peel her eyes away, it took a second for her to see that it was apparently Matt's doppelgänger. The eyes were a different color and this guy was taller, broader in the shoulders. And this guy had an air of danger. Not the scary serial killer kind, more a bad boy searching for his next heartbreak. The confidence of the man was nothing short of impressive.

Oh, baby, you can break my heart any day.

His almost perfect face had been marred with a pink scar on his lip. The small imperfection sent Mariska's curious mind into hyperdrive. Had he been protecting someone? Was he one of those guys who worked in fight clubs for a living? Muay Thai fighters were a dime a dozen in Bangkok. More than anything she itched to run her thumb across the spot and kiss it. Her pelvis tightened and her breath caught on the thought of touching him.

Lust, much?

Turning his cerulean eyes toward her, he smiled.

Holy crap. She gave a tiny gasp. He was panty-melting hot. It had been too long since she'd spent time with a man like him. Damn if she didn't want to whisk him up to her hotel room right that minute. The idea of plastering herself against his frame made her squirm on the bar stool.

Can you say stalker? You're here for business, Mar. Get a grip.

She chewed on her lip. Maybe if she could settle the case fast.

Before the solitude of the beach, I could get into some serious trouble with that guy.

She tore her eyes away and concentrated on her glass of sparkling water.

When he sat down beside her, she almost choked. Coughing, she turned to look at him.

"I'm sorry I'm late," he apologized. "I hope you weren't waiting long."

I've been waiting all my life. Mariska cocked her head as if she couldn't believe it. "Mr. Thomas?"

He watched her briefly and then smiled. "Yes." He stuck out his hand. "Were you expecting someone else?"

The warmth of him sent a thrill of anticipation through her as she put her hand in his. "No, sorry, I was distracted." *By your awesome hotness.* "I'm Mariska Stonegate. Thank you for meeting me."

"It's no problem, and it's lovely to meet you." His eyes held hers as if he had nothing better to do than gaze at her.

After a long silence, she realized she'd been staring. Reluctantly taking her hand from his, she sat up a little straighter. "I'm sorry, you weren't what I was expecting."

Something flickered in his eyes. "What do you mean?"

Embarrassed she'd actually said the words out loud, she waved a hand as if to whisk the thoughts away. "It doesn't matter. Have you found out any more information? I read your report about Mr. Gladstone not sleeping in his bed and that his luggage was still in his room. He'd called his wife earlier that day when he landed and told her he was fine, so I'm not sure what to think—"

The bartender walked up to ask what he wanted to drink. Mr. Thomas ordered the same thing as Mariska and his attention moved back to her. "You were saying?"

"That I had the information you'd e-mailed earlier. May I ask your opinion? What do you think happened to Mr. Gladstone? Has he run off with a mistress or do you suspect foul play. The police weren't very forthcoming when I asked if there might have been other businessmen who have gone missing."

Nodding, he leaned forward. "It happens in this country more often than anyone will admit. That's why it's always good to travel with a companion. It's an amazing city, but strange things happen here all the time. People disappear, never to be found again."

"Hmm. My mind was set on a different direction where Gladstone was concerned." Mariska wasn't sure how to broach the next question, but they were both professionals so she decided to lay it out there. "I'm wondering if—you know, a lonely businessman traveling to an exotic locale—if he…" She could feel her cheeks turn pink. She was far from a prude, but this subject was tough to talk about with a complete stranger.

"If perhaps he took in a bit of the local color? Visiting one of the many establishments where a man such as himself could possibly relieve some stress," he said, picking up her train of thought.

She laughed at that. "I'm not sure I could have put it so delicately, but yes, that's what I'm asking."

He glanced over her shoulder. "I see my associate. Please excuse me. I'll be right back."

Mariska didn't want to spy, but she couldn't help watching as he prowled across the bar. There was something about the way his body moved like a big cat stalking prey. At the entryway he spoke with a white-haired Asian gentleman wearing a panama hat and holding a file folder. Mr. Thomas handed the man some bills, and the older gentleman gave him the folder.

The bartender delivered the drink and she paid for it. As Thomas approached her again, he read through the file. Sitting down without glancing up from the paperwork.

That must be some interesting reading. "Your drink is here." She pointed to the glass when he sat down.

"Thanks," he said, without looking up from the file. "My associate brought me some news about *our* Mr. Gladstone." He frowned as he glanced up at her. "It's as I suspected. Mr. Gladstone asked the bellman to recommend a good place for a sauna and massage."

"Is that such a bad thing? After an eighteen-hour flight it sounds like a great idea to me." As soon as she said the words she regretted them. "Oh, a *massage.*"

"Exactly." Mr. Thomas's right eyebrow rose.

Embarrassed didn't begin to describe how she felt. She really did need to pay better attention. The last thing she wanted was to make a fool of herself in front of this guy. "Sorry, I'm a little slow today. Couldn't sleep on the plane. So, do we have a location?"

"The bellman gave him several options, but had no idea which one Mr. Gladstone chose."

Mar pursed her lips. "Hmm. Well, I guess I'd better check them all. At least I have a lead now. I should get started."

He looked at her as if she had jumped off the crazy train. "I don't think it's a good idea for you to go off on your own."

"Do you have a problem with that?" She'd run across her share of chauvinistic males. It happened a lot in the investigative business, but she was disappointed that Mr. Thomas didn't think she could do the job. His hunk factor went down at least a third. She didn't care how big his muscles were, or that her fingers had an urge to run through his hair.

He held up his hands in surrender. "No, not at all. I know for a fact women are as capable as men, many times more so. I also know your mostly female agency has a highly successful closed-case ratio." At her surprised look he explained. "I do my homework, Ms. Stonegate. I had to make sure you were a legitimate organization before agreeing to help with your case.

"What I meant was that you shouldn't go to these places alone. I'm sure you can handle yourself, but as I mentioned before, it's best to have a companion while traveling in Bangkok if at all possible. I'll escort you, no additional fee required."

Mariska was once again embarrassed for jumping to a conclusion. "That's generous of you, but I'd feel more comfortable compensating you for your time." She sounded so calm and professional. Inside she was jumping up and down like a teenager who'd met her favorite heartthrob.

It's going to be such a drag having to spend a few more hours with the hottest guy I've met in a really long time.

She almost laughed out loud. When this case was over she did need a good long break. And sex. She needed a lot of sex. Maybe then she wouldn't want to jump the first cute guy to come along.

He checked his watch. "It will be a few more hours before the bars and massage parlors open. Is there something you'd like to do until then?"

Mariska's mind went straight to a naughty place and she had to make herself not glance down at his groin.

She leaned toward him. "Yes, as a matter of fact, I'd like to go to bed."

2

JACKSON COULDN'T believe his luck. Mariska Stonegate landing in his lap was a gift. That they'd both ended up in the same hotel bar looking for information was nothing short of divine intervention. He'd have to thank the universe the first chance he had. Of course right then he had to concentrate on keeping his pants from tenting.

He knew what she meant by the "bed" comment. She'd arrived in Thailand after an eighteen-hour flight, but parts of his body weren't as understanding as his brain. Shifting in his seat, he imagined a nice cold shower.

It wasn't easy, since Mariska Stonegate was beyond enticing. Long legs poked out of a flowered skirt, and he'd even noticed her dark red toenails. Curves in all the right places and her eyes—he'd never seen a shade of green so light they were almost translucent. Her curly hair had been pulled back in a haphazard ponytail, giving her the look of a college coed on summer break.

Jackson knew better. She was intelligent and obviously damn good at what she did. Even in his business he was aware of SIA. They worked in every part of the world. Then there was the fact that her mother, Janice Stonegate, was a legendary operative. That last name had been his first clue that Mariska was someone who could help. He wondered if she even knew her mother had ever been in the CIA, before quitting to open up her own security and investigative firm.

People in his business knew about Janice, because she was one of the few international operatives to transition into civilian life successfully. She'd been killed in a plane crash last year, and many wondered if, after thirty years away, her past had finally caught up with her.

Jackson couldn't believe his luck in running into her daughter. When he'd walked into the bar he'd been looking for an ally. Dawson, his handler, said he was sending a friend. Dawson had a history of using women to convey messages, and she was the only one there. When he heard her last name, he knew he'd hit the mark.

She might not even know that she was the "friend," but she would have resources, something Jackson was seriously low on at the moment.

She seemed like a genuinely nice woman. It was unfortunate he had to pull her into his plan, but he had no choice. If it made Jackson a lying bastard, so be it.

For once, luck certainly seemed to be on his side. When he discovered Mr. Thomas was a private investigator, Jackson had slipped right into the role. Mariska was an asset in his world, and he needed her more than she could ever imagine. The fact that the image of those gorgeous eyes and generous lips would now be burned into his brain complicated things, but he had to stay on task.

When the real Mr. Thomas had walked into the bar, Jackson knew exactly who he was. The wary eyes that searched the room made him easy to pick out. He had the look of a man who had seen too much. Jackson sometimes saw the same thing when he glanced at a mirror.

The old man had fallen for the "assistant act," when Jackson told the private investigator that he worked for Ms. Stonegate. It was amazing how a few hundred dollars could make someone accept even the flimsiest of explanations. Mr. Thomas hadn't batted an eye. He'd handed over the documents, which had helped bring Jackson up to speed on the case.

The papers he held gave Jackson an easy in. The break he needed to become a part of Mariska's world. He'd help her find Mr. Gladstone. It was the least he could do. Then he'd use Mariska and her resources for his own agenda.

He coughed to cover the long pause and then gave her his most seductive grin. "If you're asking me up to your room for a bit of physical exertion—"

She laughed, her hands flitting about nervously. For an experienced P.I., she seemed so flustered around him. He appreciated the fact that she wasn't jaded like most of the people in her business.

"I so did not mean that the way it came out," she said. "I meant, I need a nap, which is more than obvious." She rolled her eyes. "I'm not sure what it is about you that ties up my tongue."

He allowed himself a second to think about her

tongue circling his... *Damn*. He really would need that cold shower if he didn't stop thinking about her that way.

"I am wondering if you could satisfy my curiosity about something." Thankfully she interrupted his thoughts again. "You don't seem like the kind of guy who would be a private investigator in Bangkok."

Huh. She was perceptive. Shrugging, he told her the truth. "I'm not." At her sharp intake of breath he added, "I'm more of a consultant, and I don't live here full-time. Bangkok is a temporary home until I clear some cases of my own.

"You know the rules about client confidentiality, but I can assure you they are along the same lines as what you are working on. That's why I thought it might be a good idea if we pooled our resources. I've spent a great deal of time here and know the city and its people well. I promise to be nothing but an asset to you."

Everything he said was true. When he'd been burned he'd been working on a human trafficking ring out of Rayong. Vlad's organization did much more than gun-running. Jackson had managed to get inside the operation and he'd made progress. But somewhere along the line Jackson had screwed things up royally, and now he'd spend whatever life he had left finding out where he'd gone wrong. Once the Company, or worse, Vlad's assassins, found him, he was a dead man.

Mariska studied him for several minutes. She was intelligent, and not easily fooled. He'd managed to use his rusty flirting skills to distract her but that would only last so long.

He glanced at his watch again to change the subject.

"We have a few hours for you to rest. I can pick you up at, say, ten? We can grab a quick bite and then head off to our first stop." It would also give him time to re-search the case and Mariska. He wondered if the SIA's resources were why Dawson had set it up so that he'd find her.

Picking up the folder, he read. "Liu Mae's Sauna and Massage is probably the best place to start. I've heard—" he pursed his lips, not wanting to go into details "—a few things about that establishment from some of my contacts."

"What kind of things?" She fingered the handle on her bag.

The narrowing of her eyes made him think she might be suspicious of something he said, but he couldn't imagine what. So he told her the truth. "That the women there get paid a great deal of money to do special favors for their clientele. Let's say there are no boundaries."

She scrunched up her nose. "Please tell me no ani-mals are involved. I'm all for sex any way you like it, but if there's a donkey, I'm so outta there." She laughed. "I can't believe I said that out loud."

The "sex any way you like it" comment caused his pants to bulge and he painfully crossed his legs to hide the evidence. His mind had flashed to a dangerous place where he had her up against a wall with her legs wrapped around him. "I don't think you have to worry about that sort of extreme, though you may see some tools of the trade," he teased her.

Standing, she pulled her bag onto her shoulder. "I don't think I even want to know what you mean. Give me a couple of hours to crash, and I'll meet you in the lobby." Holding out her hand, she waited for him to do the same. "It's been a pleasure," she said as he took her hand in his.

Her fingers were long and tapered and the skin soft against his calluses. Jackson held on a little too long. When she looked down at their hands linked together, he let go. Then she turned on her heels and walked out.

Believe me, the pleasure was all mine. Jackson watched as the lower half of him still fought for control.

He noticed three other men entering the bar glance at her as she left. A strange sensation came over him. A protective feeling that was quite unfamiliar.

Mine. He desired her in a bad way.

The instinct to punch them for staring at her was strong, but he stayed put. As he watched her hips sway under the flowery dress, how could he blame them for looking? There was a freshness, no, an innocence about her that he hadn't come across in a really long time, an unusual trait in her line of work.

Jackson chugged his mineral water. It was really too bad he didn't have time for that cold shower. He pulled out his wallet but the bartender waved him away.

"The lady already paid," the man said as he picked up Jackson's glass and wiped the bar.

Lucky for him he'd kept the folder. He'd have some time to do a bit of footwork on his own.

He also had to see a man about a passport. If he were ever going to get out of this godforsaken city, he'd need a couple of new identities.

Before that happened, he had a mess to clean up.
When he found out who had sent him on this one-way
road to hell, he'd kill them.

3

MAR WAS DETERMINED to not act like an idiot when she saw Mr. Thomas later that evening. She lay in her bed surprised that she'd been able to sleep for a couple of hours. The alarm on her cell had chimed her awake, and now she had a half hour to shower and change.

Yawning, she stretched and moved her legs to the side of the bed, wishing she could sleep a few more hours. Finally, she pushed herself up and went into the well-appointed bathroom. The Four Seasons never skimped when it came to linens or bathrooms. She turned on the hot water and thought about her meeting with Mr. Thomas.

"What kind of detective am I that I don't even know his first name? I talked to him for almost an hour." She stared at herself in the mirror wondering how much longer she could hold up this charade.

The problem was, she was no detective. Not really. Everything she knew she'd learned from studying for her Ph.D. in clinical psychology with an emphasis on the criminal mind, and researching case files at the office.

She was nothing more than a figurehead, though so far she'd been able to fool most of the agency's clients.

Two years ago she was well on her way to becoming an FBI profiler, at least that was her dream. That had changed with her mother's death.

Sad, since her mother was one of the best in the business. Of course, her mom, the founder of SIA, had also been a CIA agent, a fact Mar had only discovered a few months ago while digging through some private papers.

When she confronted her father about it, he'd said, "That part of her life was over long before you were born, hon. We don't discuss it."

Mar had tried to press him for more, but it was useless.

Obviously, Mar hadn't picked up any of her mother's special interrogation skills, because she'd let the matter fall.

She *was* good at subterfuge. She'd not only fooled the clients, but also several people at SIA headquarters. At first, when she fumbled and stumbled they believed she was still mourning her mother. She was lucky that a few of her friends, Chi, Katie and a couple of others knew the truth. They helped to hide the fact that she was in way over her head.

When it looked like everyone might figure out what was going on, she'd solved the case of a missing child by sheer luck. Mariska had been coming back from a trip to Houston when she'd stopped at a roadside barbeque joint for some ribs. There was a little girl alone in the restroom washing her hands. When Mariska saw her, she knew that it was Maddie Lennon, who had been missing for three weeks. There'd been Amber alerts and everything.

She'd checked the stalls to make sure the little girl was alone and then locked the bathroom door so no one could get in. Trying to be as calm as possible she told Maddie that she was a detective like on TV, and that she was safe. Maddie didn't say a word but she didn't try to run away. Mariska pulled out her phone and called the police.

The woman and man who'd taken the little girl had nearly beaten down the door until Mariska had shouted the police were on the way. The couple hadn't made it to the restaurant's entrance before the owner of the place pulled a shotgun and had them down on their knees. God, you had to love Texans. Later he told Mariska he knew that when they were willing to leave a child behind they were up to no good.

When the police arrived they took the couple into custody and Mar's hands were shaking so bad she almost couldn't unlock the door.

A few hours after that Maddie had been reunited with her parents. It was a happy ending and Mar was more determined than ever to be better at her new job. She studied the case files of the other investigators and brought in some of her best friends to work with the agency.

While she had no illusions that she would ever be a great investigator like her mother, she wanted to be legitimately useful. This assignment in Bangkok was a way to test herself even if she'd much rather be on vacation.

Now she was going into the underworld of a dangerous city with a sexy guy who had more secrets than she could ever imagine. Oh, she might not be the world's greatest detective but she could read people. Mr. Thomas was hiding something, though her gut told her he was sincere in wanting to help her.

There was something about the man that made her heat from the inside out. She'd seen, and even dated, plenty of hot guys. None of them had pulled at her the way he did. None of them had ever quite caused her stomach to twitter with a fiery glance. Or made her tongue do crazy somersaults so that every sentence she spoke was an effort.

She blew out a big breath and stepped into the shower.

What she really needed to do was get her libido under control. After standing under the hot water for a few minutes and soaping off she turned the tap to cold.

"Brrrr." Her teeth chattered.

It was amazing how frigid water could make a girl's body behave. She had to concentrate on the case. *Solve this one and you get a vacation. Then you can go back to being a figurehead behind your nice safe desk, in your nice safe office, researching cases for the other detectives.*

Her mind wandered to Mr. Thomas.

Maybe she didn't want to be safe any more.

"IT'S PROBABLY BEST IF we act like a couple looking for a good time," Jackson said. Over a steamy bowl of Pho noodles she'd finally learned his name.

He took her hand in his as they walked down the street. She knew it was to protect her from the throng of people here in the red light district. She'd been a lot of places, but none as crowded as this. Well, maybe Times Square on New Year's. But this wasn't any special day. Between those in storefronts hawking their wares to street vendors with chickens and lizards hanging from their stalls, it was nothing short of overwhelming.

I don't think I'll be trying the lizard.

As his fingers wrapped around hers it was so easy for her to pretend that they belonged together. In the last hour over dinner her determination to be professional had wavered. He'd arranged it so they had a quiet table and that she had everything she needed. It was as if he were taking care of her.

At any other time she might have been annoyed with a man ordering for her, but with Jackson, well, he was different. Not only did he have a thorough knowledge of the language, he was in tune with her taste. The noodles were exactly what she wanted. The right hint of heat and curry.

"For someone who doesn't live here, you certainly know how to speak Thai. You guys were talking so fast I couldn't even pick up one of the few words I know."

Jackson squeezed her hand, and the warmth seemed to spread through her limbs. This guy did things to her like no other.

"I travel a great deal and pick up languages as I go," he said. "I guess some might say I have an affinity for it."

They were on a busy street in the Banglampu district and only a few blocks from their destination. The small talk was Mar's way of easing her nerves. She had let Jackson become a distraction and that was far from a good thing, especially since she had no idea what she would do once they arrived at the sauna and massage parlor.

Should I question the owner? Try to find out if they've ever seen or heard of Mr. Gladstone? That didn't seem such a smart idea since people in these kinds of places valued confidentiality.

Mar wasn't so naive that she didn't know a couple of hundred dollars in the right hands could buy all the information she needed. That's why she had more than a thousand tucked under her bra in a special pouch. The problem was how to know which palm to grease. That's something they didn't teach in the textbooks.

I should have called Katie and asked her what questions to pose. I don't have a clue what I'm supposed to do once we get in there.

As they turned the corner she saw the neon sign. Her stomach churned.

Be a big girl and do the job. Follow procedure.

Thanks to her degree, and the studying and observing she'd done the last year, maybe she could at least fake her way through this thing. *Gather the information.* It was an easy first step. Mar almost snorted at that.

Jackson stopped halfway down the block and turned to her. "Are you okay? You seem nervous."

"Nervous?" She repeated his words because she wasn't sure what to say. As far as he knew she was a seasoned professional, a jaded detective who did this sort of thing all the time. "Of course not. Still a little jet-lagged." *Liar.* "I'm trying to determine the best course of action. Deep thoughts and all that." *Shut up. Deep thoughts? What the hell am I saying?*

Eyeing her curiously, he smiled. "Like I said before, it's probably best to act like we're together. If you don't mind, I'll take the lead. I'll ask for a couples massage, then we can tag team them."

At that her eyes snapped up. *Naked? In a room with Jackson? Oh, my.* "Sure, I'll take your lead on this. You know the area and the people better than I do." Her voice came out as a whisper.

"It will probably be easier to get information if we have a couple of the girls alone. While we're getting the massage we'll try to talk to them."

Sounded like a great plan to Mar—one where she didn't make an idiot of herself by running back to her hotel to hide under the covers. She would never do that, but she'd thought about it more than once throughout the evening.

There was one big problem in giving up—Stonegate had a one hundred percent success rate on closing cases and she refused to be the one to screw that up.

No. You will pay attention and help Jackson get the information you need. Pretend. Like theater class, assume the role of the doting wife. I'll imagine he's the man of my dreams—okay, that won't be such a stretch.

Since he knew the language, Jackson would be doing most of the talking and she could follow along like a good little puppy. No one need ever know she was a terrified neophyte.

This might work out well after all.

"Great," she murmured as they passed through the

door into the tacky reception area. Deep red walls overpowered the small space and there were golden statuettes on every available surface. The art on the walls was of nude Asian women pleasuring themselves in a variety of positions. The place was one giant cliché, exactly what she thought of when she imagined a Bangkok massage parlor.

Mar swallowed hard and concentrated on the old woman behind the high desk.

"You American?" she said in English.

"Yes." Jackson gave her a devastating grin.

She looked him up and down as if he were a piece of beef for sale. "Prices here." She pointed up at a board behind her.

If Mar's currency exchange rates were right in her head, this would be a cheap night. Couples massage was listed in Thai, French and English, and it was only a hundred. There was a dash and then, EXTRAS $200 American Dollars.

Mar didn't want to think about what *EXTRAS* meant.

"We want the couples massage. No extras," Jackson told the woman.

That last comment caused her to choke, and Mar stifled a cough with her hand.

"You pay first." The old woman stuck out her hand.

Jackson pulled out some bills, making sure to separate a twenty to tip the older woman.

She winked at him and then pushed a button so that a door to their left opened. "Third door. Green one.

You undress then push button by bed. Girls there in a minute."

Undress? Mar's hands trembled and she stuffed them into the pockets of her jeans. As she followed Jackson down the hall, she seriously wondered why she'd thought it a good idea to catch dinner before they began investigating. Her stomach didn't seem to want to play nice, and it gurgled in a not-so-sexy fashion.

Taking a deep breath, she moved through the door when he held it open for her.

This room was a bit more Zen than the entry. There were two massage tables with what looked like clean sheets and blankets. There was a place on the back side of the door to hang clothing. Two candles burned on a shelf with a variety of bottled oils.

Jackson unbuttoned his shirt and hung it on one of the hooks.

Mar gasped. The man was beyond gorgeous. Well-defined muscles on his back led down to narrow hips. What intrigued her the most were the scars. She was no expert but more than one looked like it had come from a bullet.

He glanced back to look at her. "Sorry, I wasn't thinking. Nudity doesn't bother me like it does some people. I'll get undressed and then lay down so you'll have some privacy."

Mar's hands waved madly of their own volition. "It's no big deal. We're professionals doing what it takes to get the job done. And if we get a great massage in the process, who's complaining?" The words were lame even to her but she couldn't seem to shut up.

"So are we expected to strip all the way down?" She

turned her back as Jackson unzipped his jeans. "I'm not sure if I should wear my underwear or not. I never am. It's crazy. I get massages all the time, but I've never had the courage to ask." She kept blathering on, to her own chagrin.

She heard him move. "I suppose it depends on the client and their level of modesty. Doesn't bother me. My lower back's giving me trouble so I'm losing the shorts. Okay, I'm on the table. I'll keep my head to the wall until you are under the sheets."

Mar glanced over at the table and her body trembled with need. The man was nothing short of a god in her book. The sheet barely covered his lower half and she could see the outline of the world's most perfect butt. He was bronze and beautiful.

Head in the game. He's going to think you're some kind of perv if you keep staring at him like he's a meal. She forced her fingers to pull the T-shirt she'd been wearing over her head. Then she lost the jeans, bra and finally the pink lacy thong. She'd never once had a massage completely nude. This would be an entirely new experience for her in more ways than one.

Hurrying, she slid under the cool sheets. "Okay. I'm ready."

Jackson turned toward her. "It's going to be fine, I promise."

"I know," she said. "This is a bit unorthodox. I mean are we going to have to use the services of everyone we interview?"

Jackson chuckled. "That would be entertaining but time-consuming. No, it's this place that caters to a certain level of clientele. I have a hunch we may find something out here. Don't ask me why, but I always follow my hunches."

It was a hell of a lot more than what she had to go on. "Well, what's the worst that can happen? We get a massage. I've had worse assignments." Not really, but she could at least pretend she had.

"You said it." There was sadness, and perhaps a touch of deep regret in his voice, which made her look at him more closely. He sounded as if he'd been through hell.

Jackson pushed the buzzer and Mar took a big breath. This was going to be one to share with the girls back at the office. They'd crack up when they heard that she was naked in a room with a man getting a massage. She could almost hear Katie's "Yeah, right. You had to get naked with a hot guy, and get a massage—for the job. Why can't I get those kinds of cases?" Mariska smiled. Yes, her friend would give her a hard time, but if this worked and she found Gladstone, she'd also be proud of her.

Katie had made it her sole mission to protect Mariska, and to help her through one of the toughest times of her life when her mother had died. But that didn't keep her best friend from joking with her.

Mar clasped her hands under her chin. She needed to focus. She didn't want Jackson to think she was some kind of amateur.

You are an amateur. Yes, but he doesn't have to know that.

She stole one more glance and found him smiling at her.

"Ready?" he said as the door opened.

No. She smiled back at him. *What in the hell am I doing?*

4

As Jackson watched the masseuse run her hands along Mariska's spine he had trouble concentrating on what they needed to accomplish here. *It's all about the job.* He couldn't think about her dewy soft skin, and the way Mariska moaned slightly when the woman hit a particular spot between her shoulders.

Did she make that sound during sex? It didn't help that the room was filled with a spicy sandalwood scent from the candles and the oil. He wondered what it would be like if his hands caused that tiny but extremely effective noise.

For the life of him, he couldn't remember why he thought a couples massage was such a great idea. Thanks to her moans it would be a while before he would be able to flip to his backside.

His purpose upon entering the room had been to chat up the two women working on them, but they refused to talk. It was almost as if they'd been told to keep quiet.

Mariska turned her head toward him and gave a sweet smile. "Honey, this was such a wonderful idea."

Mariska sighed happily. "I'm so glad your friend Mr. Gladstone recommended it."

The tiny woman who'd been running her hands up and down his body had climbed up onto the table and held on to a large wire mounted to the ceiling as she used her feet to do the work of untying the knots in his back. At the mention of Mr. Gladstone, she'd paused.

"I'll have to remember to thank him when I see him," Jackson said. The repetitive footwork began again. "He must be busy with his meeting, since he hasn't called yet. He was supposed to contact me this morning, but no one has heard from him."

"Oh." Mariska had thrown some worry into her voice. "I hope he's okay."

Jackson shot a glance at the woman working on Mariska and saw that she had a frown on her face, as if she was about to say something but thought better of it. He wondered if she had been the one to give Gladstone his massage.

"Me, too," Jackson added. "He was going to suggest a club for us to visit, too. Said it was wild, but I told him we like to step out of our comfort zone when we travel. You know how much I want to play cards while we're here. I know there has to be some action somewhere, but I have no idea where to look."

"Hon, you and your cards. Don't you think that money would be better spent on shoes?" She giggled, and he laughed along with her. She played the part well.

"I'm kidding. Maybe someone at the hotel, or maybe even here, will know a place we can go tonight," she said. "I want to go dancing. After this massage I'll feel all warm and sexy. Dancing with you would be so perfect. Then we'll find you a card game. What do you say, honey, are you up for it?"

Oh, I'm definitely up. Her voice deepened to a sexy soft velvet when she said the words *sexy and warm,* sending his senses into overdrive. *Calm down. She's only doing her job.* Jackson cleared his throat, but before he could answer, the woman working on Mariska chimed in.

"Best dance club is Phatong," she said in a singsong voice. "Very sexy. You wear short dress. Not very many married couple go, though. Mostly businessmen looking for women and if you ask right people you can find card—"

The woman working on his back hissed as if to shush the other one.

The girl walking on Mariska's back shrugged. Jackson found the interplay between the two women interesting. He couldn't tell if the older woman didn't want the younger one to share information, or if she was concerned for Mariska and him.

"Oh, that sounds like fun. Thank you," Mariska said. "We love dancing. Then maybe we can, um, find those people she talked about so you can play cards, honey." Mariska was definitely getting into their charade.

From the toe action down his spine Jackson thought the woman walking on top of him might be angry. If she dug into his shoulder one more time, he might have to take her out. It hadn't completely healed from the beating he'd received from Vlad's men a few months ago.

It appeared to him as if Phatong would be the best

place to continue their search for Gladstone. He'd seen the club a couple of days ago when he quickly toured the red light district searching for one of his old contacts. Of course, the man was nowhere to be found. It was no coincidence that anyone who could have possibly helped Jackson seemed to have disappeared.

She jumped off the table and patted his shoulder. "I do front now." That was her way of ordering him to flip over. Jackson considered it for a moment and realized his thinking about Vlad had rid his mind of all the sexy thoughts from before.

All he had to do was try and not look at or listen to the sensual Mariska.

BEFORE THEY HIT THE CLUB, Mariska begged to take a quick shower to get the heavy oils off her skin and to change into something more appropriate for club hopping.

Jackson followed her to the room. As she turned on the water he tried his best not to think about her soaping herself up as the warm water sprayed the oil off her sexy body. The very idea caused his gut to tighten with pleasure.

Sitting down at the desk in front of the large expanse of windows, he didn't have time to take in the view of the city lights. He made a few quick phone calls to the front desk, and to hotel security pretending to be Mariska's assistant again. Once he had completed his tasks, he did his best to concentrate on the background check on the club.

Borrowing her laptop, he was able to get the information he needed by doing some quick searches. As he suspected, the club was a front for a busy casino in the red light district, one that wasn't that well hidden. Jackson hoped they would find some clues about what happened to Gladstone.

Jackson hadn't lied about hunches. As soon as the women at the massage parlor mentioned the club, he thought perhaps their quarry might be a gambler. There hadn't been anything in the file about Gladstone having a penchant for cards, but it would explain the long absence from his hotel. More than likely he'd been on the hunt for a card game, too, and that's why the younger girl had mentioned it. If she'd been working on the other man, there was a good chance she'd mentioned the same place.

The club would be a good start, but they might have to hit a few clubs to find their man. Then again, they might get lucky. Though, until he'd run into Mariska earlier, luck hadn't exactly been on Jackson's side the last few months.

On to more important matters. He thanked the stars that Mariska had exactly the software he needed to implement the second part of his plan. Using an untraceable account, he sent an e-mail to Dawson.

Jackson had no idea if the other agent would even read it, but it was worth a chance. A few weeks ago Dawson said he was looking into what happened to Jackson, and that he'd help find out how he'd been burned, but so far they'd both come up with nothing. One minute his cover was blown, the next he'd been burned. His fist tightened on the keyboard and he forced himself to relax.

Thanks for the asset. She is something. News? He

typed the words using the code he and Dawson had devised, hitting send as the water shut off.

What he really wanted to ask was, why Mariska? While her laptop and resources would definitely come in handy, there didn't seem much she could do for him. Well, she was obviously loaded. Maybe Dawson thought he could use the cash. And possibly use spending time with her as a cover. No one would look for a burned CIA agent with a wealthy socialite.

Jackson picked up the phone and called the front desk to get a car and make some arrangements in case they found their quarry.

Mariska hummed a sweet tune in the bathroom and it was more than a little distracting. It took everything he had not to offer to dry her off. It had been a long time since his mind had been so full of a woman, probably not since one of his high school crushes.

He brought up the search engine again, and cleared away any evidence of what he'd been doing before. He didn't want to risk suspicion.

When she walked out of the bathroom, she might as well have roundhouse kicked him in the gut. Her long, tan legs were at the bottom of a short black skirt topped with a red halter that looked sexy, but not cheap. Her feet were in sexy heels and it took him a minute to catch his breath.

She stared at him, scrunching up her nose. "Is everything all right?" Twirling around, she flashed a hand down her outfit. "Do you think it's too much? I thought it would be best if I looked like arm candy, but do you think I need more makeup or something?"

She said it as if she had no idea how much the total

package would be a constant distraction for him. Hell, she'd be a distraction for any man. Mar didn't seem to have any idea how gorgeous she was, and he found that extremely appealing.

"No." He shook his head. "I meant—the outfit is fine. I have some information for you." He told her about the casino as she searched the dresser drawers for something.

"There's one little problem. I'm not exactly flush with cash right now and to get in we're going to need some to blow on the kind of game we want," Jackson admitted. He did have a stash, but he had no idea how long it would have to last him.

She pulled out a purse from the dresser and put a lipstick and some other things inside. "Oh, that's no problem. I brought some extra cash." She pursed her lips as she walked toward him and he forced himself to stand still, instead of leaning forward and kissing the plum-colored softness before him. "Do you think twenty thousand will be enough? I can get more if we need it."

The thousand-dollar-a-night suite was his first clue that she had money, but who traveled with that much cash?

"That should get us into the good tables," he said, choking back a laugh.

"Cool." She looked down at her outfit again, pulling at a thread. "Um, I don't exactly have anywhere to carry that much, so maybe you better hold on to it."

He realized how much she trusted him and a small pit of guilt opened up in Jackson's gut. He didn't deserve it, and when she found out, if she found out, who he really was she would hate him for eternity. But for now, he'd help her with her job, and do his best to keep her happy. If he helped her solve her case, there was a great chance she'd feel indebted to him. That might come in handy over the next week or so.

She seemed confident in her skin, but unaware of her beauty. Then there was her job. When it came down to tracking Gladstone, she really did seem clueless. It didn't add up.

As they entered the lobby, he couldn't resist asking. "Do you always travel with that much cash?"

She rolled her eyes. "You must think I'm insane. No. The bank delivered the money to the hotel this morning. Part of it is expenses for this case. I didn't know how long it would take, and informants don't take credit." She fiddled with the purse.

Pausing for a moment, she seemed to check herself. "And part of it was for shopping. I planned to have clothes designed for myself, and some friends, and most of the tailors only accept cash. I have this, um, sort of compulsion for silk suits, and they make beautiful ones here."

Jackson still thought that was a lot of money for a wardrobe, but he wasn't one to judge. For him, money was a necessary evil of his job. Money equaled power, and he'd seen so many misuse both in his line of work. At least she was only buying clothes and not guns, which is what most of the people he'd worked with the last few years did.

After checking the cash out of the safe downstairs they climbed into the hired car Jackson had ordered from her hotel room. Taxis weren't always safe in

Bangkok, and he decided to rent a hired car in case they needed a quick getaway.

The club wasn't far, but the traffic congestion was intense even close to midnight.

"Is it always like this here?" Mariska asked as she stared out at the crowds on the sidewalk.

"Pretty much 24/7," Jackson replied. "It really is a city that never sleeps. The massage parlor was at the edge of the red light district, but this place is dead center. There's—" He stopped suddenly, trying to think of the best way to tell her.

She gave him a curious look as if she wasn't really ready for more surprises. He was sorry he had to disappoint her. "What?"

"I guess the easiest way to say this is, be ready for anything. You never know what you're going to see in these clubs. It's okay to act surprised, that's what they expect from tourists, which is what we'll be for our cover. If that's okay with you."

She fidgeted in her seat. "Do you think there will be snakes?" Her voice had gone soft again and his body reacted.

"I don't know what you mean?" Jackson really was clueless.

"In the club. I saw this movie one time where these people danced with the huge snakes. I'm not a big fan of reptiles. They give me the squiggles."

Jackson couldn't help but laugh, and accidentally knocked his elbow against the door of the car.

"Um, I can't say for sure, but I don't remember seeing anything about snakes when I did the research."

"Okay. Good. No snakes." She took a deep breath and her face relaxed.

He couldn't believe that snakes were the things she was most worried about. The truth was they were probably going to run into more than one snake of the human variety, but that's why he was there. He'd protect her.

The car stopped in the middle of the street, and Jackson saw the flashing lights to the right. "Ah, here we are."

The music booming out of the club was so loud they could hear it from in the car with the windows rolled up. Jackson slipped the driver an extra hundred and told him to hang around the corner on a different street. Then he paused and looked back through the window. "The hotel should have a package ready for you. Put it in the trunk and then we'll meet up with you soon."

"Okay," the driver told him.

Phatong was one of those glossy-on-the-surface places with silver walls and glass tables, but underneath that it was slick and seedy. The loud music and the decor had been designed to make people drink. The more they danced, the more they drank. The more the clientele imbibed, the more likely they were to lose money in the casino.

Jackson had a plan. Keeping his hand on Mariska's back, he led her to the dance floor. "This is the easiest place for us to get a good run of the place. Keep an eye out and let me know if you see any muscle. That's most likely where we'll find the casino entrance. They'll have some guards posted to keep out any cops who might wander in. Best not to rush these things. We'll let them think we're here for a good time."

Smiling up at him, she nodded. That show of pearly white teeth against the plum lips was enough for his cock to stir again. This had to stop.

She is a means to an end.

This was a job like so many he'd done before. He had to stay alert and couldn't think about things like how her body would feel next to his.

The crowd around them was a mix of tourists and young locals hitting the club scene. The fast electronica beat moved into a slow song as they hit the dance floor.

Damn. Now he was about to find out exactly how she felt tight against him. At least he didn't have to bop around like an idiot to fast music. That was one thing he'd never picked up in his training. The waltz and a modified box step were about all he could handle.

Of course, there was also the slow high school move where you put your arms around her waist and moved back and forth. Unfortunately for his libido, that was the only kind of dancing that fit this particular song. He pulled her to him in a smooth move, wrapping his arms around her hips, his hands lightly touching her lower back.

Her arms slid around his neck, and he tried not to think about her pert breasts pushing into his chest or the seductive way her hips moved from side to side. No, he wasn't thinking about those things at all.

"She sure gets around," Mariska said.

Jackson glanced around. "Who?"

"Natasha Bedingfield," Mariska whispered, her breath tickling his ear and sending shivers of pleasure down his spine.

"Is she here?"

Her soft laugh caused him to gaze down at her beautiful face.

"Do you have any idea who she is?" Mar grinned at him as if he were missing the joke.

Jackson thought for a moment, but the name didn't mean anything to him. "Uh, no."

"She's singing this song, 'Soulmate,' and it happens to be one of my favorites. It's a few years old but I've always loved it."

She was talking about the music. Jackson didn't spend much time in the States, and while he had an MP3 player, he used it for downloading books, historical fiction and biographies.

"It's nice." It was an inane thing to say, but he wasn't familiar with the artist. He did make a note that it was one of Mariska's favorites. He wasn't sure exactly why he found that necessary.

Keep your mind on the job, man.

Taking in the rest of the club, he twirled her around. There were a couple of bouncers near an entrance at the back. His first instinct was to hit the bar and get an invite, but the woman in his arms made him want to hold off a few minutes more.

It's her favorite song after all. The fact that her fingers played a seductive rhythm on his neck had nothing to do with it.

When it ended, he took her hand and pushed through to the crowded bar. As he waited for the bartender to get their drinks, he listened to other patrons. One guy was talking about winning at the wheel. That meant a roulette table. They were on the right track.

Careful how he worded it, he spoke to the bartender in stilted Thai. He wanted the man to think he was a tourist who recently learned the language. Jackson asked if he knew of a place where a man could find a solid card game. Then he handed him a hundred-dollar tip. The other man pointed toward the back. "Tell them Kwan sent you."

"Okay." He pulled Mariska away from the crowd. "We're going in, but there are some ground rules. Stay close and at the first hint of trouble we are out of there."

As hard as he tried, it was tough to think of Mariska as a business partner. He had an overwhelming need to protect her. So much so that he considered scrapping their plan and taking her back to the hotel. He could handle this part of the job on his own.

"Jackson, I'm not an idiot." Mariska's frustration could be heard in her tone. "Trust me when I tell you that at the first sign of trouble I'll be booking it like nobody's business. Please don't even go there."

He glanced up to see the bartender watching them. To keep the man from getting suspicious he leaned down and captured Mariska's lips. There was a tiny "oh," from her but she didn't fight him. Her arms snuck up around his neck as he further explored her mouth. She was sweet with a slight tang of the lime from her drink. More intoxicating than any alcohol he could have imagined.

Jackson lost himself in her. His brain shut down and his body responded to her in ways he hadn't allowed himself in years.

This woman could be the death of me. The thought helped Jackson to finally pull himself away from her, but it wasn't easy. "Ready?"

5

JACKSON HAD KISSED HER. Gawd, that was amazing even for a fake kiss. Mariska's stomach was full of butterflies and even her eyes had lost focus for a second.

She glanced at the door where two bodyguards stood, and worried about what Jackson had said to her about surprises that might be behind the curtain. So far there'd been no snakes. Thank God. She'd been so embarrassed when she brought that up in the car, but snakes were definitely a deal-breaker for her.

"What exactly are you expecting to find back there?" Mariska asked the question to give herself time to check her knees and make sure they worked. She knew Jackson had only kissed her because he'd caught someone watching them. It was too sudden for anything else.

While she didn't want to admit it, the kiss had been one of the best she'd ever experienced. It would have been nice if it'd been real. Her body already craved his touch. Maybe when they finished this case she could convince him to go with her to the beach resort where she planned to vacation for a couple of weeks.

The very idea of asking a man to spend two weeks

*holed up in a beach villa. Please. What a— God, I'm
going to do it. If we make it out alive from this place,
I'm going to ask him to go with me. If he says no, I'll
live.*

She would never let on, but he'd absolutely scared the
crap out of her with his worry about what was behind
the curtain. Pretending she was worldly hadn't been
easy in that moment.

More than anything she wanted to take his hand and
run out the front entrance and to the safety of the town
car. She didn't need to find Gladstone that bad. Then all
she had to do was convince Jackson to run away to the
beach with her. That prospect was much more enticing
than going through the curtain with the two guards.

She glanced up to see Jackson was answering her
question, and she'd missed most of his answer. She
forced herself to focus.

"It's best to be on guard at all times. We're here to
gather information, nothing more. The most important
thing is, if you see Gladstone, don't let on that you know
him right away. Give me some kind of signal and then
we'll play it by ear."

Jackson squeezed her hand and she gave him her
most reassuring smile.

Jackson said something in Thai, and the guards
pulled back the curtains. The disco part of the club
hadn't prepared Mariska for the freak circus in front
of her. The casino, packed with masses of people, was
an overwhelming, nasty mess. From the flashing lights
to the totally nude cocktail waitresses, it was an assault
on the senses.

There were blackjack tables, slot machines, roulette

wheels and everything else one might find in a Vegas casino, including card games in side rooms along the casino floor.

Down the center of the casino was a line of large birdcages hanging from the ceiling. Inside were nude dancers. A few of the cages had more than one girl and they were making out. Hell, it was more than making out. It was erotic and kind of sleazy at the same time.

Note to self: Don't look up. Holy crap. Eyes forward.

The girls were a distraction so that people didn't pay attention to how much money they were losing. She knew that. Still, though Mariska had partied hard in her early college days, hitting some of the not-so-lovely bars in Austin, New Orleans, Vegas and L.A., she'd never seen anything like this.

Jackson glided in with his arm around her shoulders. The warmth of him helped her get her bearings in the sea of people. He moved as if he knew exactly where he was going. She walked beside him, and admired Jackson's way of looking like he owned the room. The man definitely didn't lack self-confidence, which was the exact opposite of how she felt.

Now that they were in, her stomach tightened with unease. She felt completely overwhelmed.

This was a dumb idea. We're never going to find him in this mess. Seconds after she thought it, she spotted Gladstone. He was across the large expanse where the slot and poker machines were lined up.

She must have tensed, because Jackson leaned down and whispered against her ear. "Where is he?"

He's good. Jackson was so in tune with everything

around him that even her slight movement caused him to take notice. She reached up and touched his cheek to help with the charade and to hide their lips as she whispered back, "Straight ahead and to the left. End chair at the big table."

Jackson hugged her, and then kissed her again, lingering a little longer than necessary for their theatrics. She didn't mind a bit.

"Good job. Now follow me." He winked at her.

Jeez, if he didn't stop touching her like that she would melt into the floor. Seriously, she'd be the wicked witch of the west in a puddle, or was that the wicked witch of the east. She could never remember.

If Jackson knew what he did to her, he'd run for his life. His touch around her shoulders sent electricity through her body, heating and teasing. Her nipples tightened, which was unfortunate since the thin halter she wore didn't hide much.

Great. They really are going to think I'm cheap eye candy.

Taking their time crossing the floor, they watched some of the tables for a few minutes. Then they stopped to play roulette, and Mariska won. "Oh, my, Gawd. This is so much fun!

"I've never been this lucky," she said as she cashed in her coins for bills. Since her purse was barely big enough to hold her phone and lipstick she handed the money to Jackson.

"That's how they pull you in," he said under his breath as he led her toward Gladstone. They were close enough now that she could see the lines of worry etched in the other man's face, shadowed by a couple of days' whisker growth. His pile of chips wasn't very high.

"My guess is he's been here for at least two days. He probably started out with a big wad of cash and now he thinks he can win it all back." Jackson took her hand in his and moved into the crowd that surrounded the table. There were four other men and the dealer playing. It was a form of poker but she didn't recognize the game.

When Jackson let go of her hand and moved forward she was shocked.

"Desmond, is that you?" Jackson had waited for a lull in the action while the dealer shuffled the cards. He stepped forward and stuck out his hand.

The other man shook it but had a look of uncertainty on his face.

Jackson carried on his ruse. "What the heck are you doing here?" He tilted his head back toward Mariska. "The little woman is here with me. Where's your wife? She was complaining this morning that I was no fun shopping, maybe the girls could spend the day together tomorrow." He glanced at his watch. "Make that later today."

Desmond Gladstone wasn't sure what to think of Jackson. She could tell from the wary look in his eyes. Bloodshot eyes that revealed he'd been at the table way too long, and it looked as if he'd had one too many drinks.

Alcohol could make a man stupid. Hell, it could make a woman stupid. She'd made plenty of mistakes after a few too many. His hair was mussed, and though he was in his early thirties according to the background report the agency sent, he appeared much older, haggard and unhealthy, as if he hadn't had a decent meal or a shower in days.

Jackson continued the charade, looking around as if trying to find the other man's wife. Gladstone took the bait.

It wasn't surprising since Jackson was so damn convincing. The man should have been a star in Hollywood for the show he put on. He acted as if he'd known Gladstone all his life, and even Mariska would have believed the scheme if she didn't know the truth.

"She's back in the States. I'm here on business." Gladstone shook his head as if he'd been in a daze, then he sat a little straighter in his chair as if to make himself look more important.

Monkey business. She couldn't help it. Gladstone's poor wife was back home worried sick and here he was in the middle of a card game. Of course if the wife had mentioned a gambling problem, it would have made the agency's job much easier.

"We were going to grab a late dinner. When do you think you'll be finished here? We'd love to catch up. Do you know it's been almost two—" Jackson was interrupted by a large man who stepped in front him.

The man barked an order, and Jackson held his hands up. "Hey, I'm only trying to say hi to an old friend." He leaned around the burly man. "We'll wait for you and then we'll head out for some dim sum."

Gladstone glanced down at his chips and a look of defeat washed over his face. "Shouldn't be long."

It wasn't.

After four more hands, Mar watched as the man slid his chips forward, calling, "All in." She held her breath, her nerves raw with anticipation. *He's a friggin' lunatic, or he has a really good hand.*

When he flipped up the three kings, she thought he'd won. Then another man at the end of the table had five spades.

Gladstone's head fell to his hands in despair.

"A flush will kill you every time," Jackson said beside her. He'd taken her hand again and she appreciated the calming effect he had on her.

That was until he motioned with his eyes to the side door. She gave a slight nod that she understood.

Oh, hell, we're making a break for it.

"Well, old man. You can't win them all," he said to Gladstone. "How about you come with us and we'll buy you some dinner. Looks to me like you could use a break from the tables."

Gladstone stared blankly ahead as if he didn't hear Jackson.

"Hey, Earth to Des. Come on, let's go eat," Jackson encouraged the man. "It's on me."

The other man finally glanced up. "Uh. Sure."

The dealer pointed a finger. "Markers?" He told Gladstone. "You have good credit here. We take care of you and you can win money back." The stilted English wasn't lost on Mar. They didn't want Gladstone to get up from the table.

The bouncer guy, who had stepped in front of Jackson, put a hand on Gladstone's shoulder. "You stay."

Jackson shifted so he was inches from the big burly man, and Mar wondered if he was getting ready to take out the bodyguard. They'd have to make a run for it if he did that, and she wasn't exactly sure she could manage it in four-inch heels. Though, with the adrenaline pumping through her veins she had a feeling she'd make a good go of it. Everyone seemed so tense, and the bodyguard looked as if he'd have no problem pummeling Jackson.

Moving two steps closer, Jackson gave the bodyguard a wink. "Hey guys, I'll bring him back, but the man needs to eat. Surely you can spare him long enough to have a quick meal with friends. I'm sure he wants a chance to win his money back."

Gladstone shrugged the guard's hand off his shoulder. "I'll be back, but I'd like to spend some time with my friends," he said to them.

"Maybe I'll even come back and play a few rounds." Jackson gave the table an affable smile. "I think I'd very much like a chance to win my friend's money back from you guys."

Gladstone stepped down from the platform where the table sat and stood beside Jackson. "Okay, buddy. Let's find us dim sum." Moving a protective arm around the other man's shoulder he used his other hand to motion Mar to walk in front of them. "Keep moving and don't stop even if the guards say something," he whispered to her.

Mar's heart went down to her gut when she saw the two large men at the door, who seemed to take a keen interest in the three of them.

Oh, my, God. We're going to die.

6

Two guards, roughly the size of sumo wresters, created a wall in front of the nearest exit. Mar had a feeling trying to shove her way through would be like trying to push down a couple of giant redwoods with her bare hands.

Crap. What do I do now?

"No," the one on the right said gruffly, his face giving new meaning to the word *menace*. She didn't know much Thai, but *no* seemed universal.

Think fast or die, crazy girl.

"But." Mar threw her hand up to her mouth as if she were going to be sick. "Had too much to drink, I'm gonna seriously hurl. Please."

They didn't budge.

Mar forced her eyes to go big and a low gagging sound came from her throat as if she were doing her best not to throw up on them. It really wasn't much of a stretch. She'd never been so scared in her life.

"Please, gentlemen, the lady doesn't want to embarrass herself here, and trust me when I tell you she definitely had too much to drink," Jackson said affably.

His hand went to her back. "She was quite the wild woman on the dance floor tonight."

The choking sound burbled from her throat again, and this time the mountain of men parted and even held the door open for them to exit.

They were out of the club and into the hired car around the corner before Gladstone even had a chance to question who they were.

Mar's nerves were on edge, so much so she had to put her hands on her knees to stop them from shaking.

Jackson shut the door behind her and sat in front with the driver so they wouldn't be crowded in the back.

Gladstone was in some kind of daze, as if he wasn't quite sure what had happened. Once the car pulled into traffic, Mar regained her strength. Taking a deep breath, she turned to face the man to her left. "Mr. Gladstone, I'm Mariska Stonegate from Stonegate Investigative Agency. I was sent by your wife to find out why you disappeared from the hotel."

"Oh." Her words seemed to sink in through his confusion. Then his eyes flashed with understanding. "Damn. She knows. God, can nothing go right tonight? She'll be royally pissed that you didn't find me dead." The unexpected response confused Mar.

Jackson grunted from his seat.

"I don't think that's true," Mar continued. "She was quite worried when she called the agency. I happened to be in the area and promised to follow up." Mariska didn't like the man, but his wife and child deserved answers.

"When she finds out I gambled away the second mortgage she is most definitely going to wish me six feet under." Gladstone raked a hand through his hair. "And I don't blame her. I was on such a roll and I thought I was going to really do it this time."

"It never happens," said Jackson, his voice low and gravelly as he turned to stare Gladstone directly in the eyes. "You need help, and you need to know that there never is a this time or a next time. You might win once or twice, or hit a lucky streak for a few hours, but when you don't know when to stop you end up losing it all. Every time."

"You don't know that," Gladstone spit out bitterly, the acid in his tone unmistakable. "I was doing okay tonight. I lost focus. That all-in play at the end—"

"Saved you a lot of heartache," Jackson interrupted. "I know what I'm talking about. My dad spent a great deal of time at the track before he died."

For a few seconds Jackson's confident mask lifted and she saw the vulnerable boy underneath. A child hurt by the people who were supposed to protect him. She had to consciously keep her hand from touching his brow so that she could soothe away the hurt she glimpsed there. A beat later the confident, steely mask returned.

"I don't have a problem. It's a run of bad luck," said Gladstone. "I know what I'm doing. I had an off night at the tables, it doesn't make me some loser with an addiction like your *dad*." The last word spewed out of his mouth full of hate.

Mar never wanted to punch a guy so bad as she did right then.

"Yes, it does. And you've been at those tables for two days at least." Jackson didn't back down. His voice had a hard edge of steel in it. Mar was grateful the words weren't directed at her. "I can tell from the way you're talking that this isn't the first time you've done this. You can't see it, but you're about to lose everything that is precious to you. The mortgage aside, if you keep gambling, your wife and child aren't going to stay in your life. You need help."

"So that's what all this is, some kind of intervention? Thanks, but no thanks. You can let me out on the corner."

Mariska's eyebrow went up. "I'm beginning to wonder why your wife wants a deadbeat like you back home." It might be a harsh thing to say, but the man needed a solid dose of truth. She had no compassion for idiots who only thought about themselves and left their families to suffer their mistakes. "You're lucky we found you. If you borrowed money from those guys, your life would be even more complicated. You didn't, by the way, borrow any money?"

Gladstone glanced out the window, not bothering to answer.

"Let me tell you something about these types of casinos," Jackson interjected. "They are run by the Thai and Russian mafia. That big guy who stepped in front of me at the table was Russian. They take your money and offer markers when you run out.

"Then you wake up the next morning after being sleep deprived for three days straight, you realize it wasn't so much bad luck as a huge screw-up because you find yourself having to pay forty percent interest on a huge loan."

Holy crap. Mar knew it would be bad but had no idea

it would be that much. Jackson must have come across this kind of thing in his line of work, or maybe with his dad. He did seem to know what he was talking about.

Gladstone stared at his hands as if they were the most interesting things in the world.

"When you can't pay, and who the hell could? They make you sign over your house." Jackson pointed a finger at the man. "Then they come after your business, telling you they only need a few shares to call it even. All of the sudden they own every aspect of your life and you are screwed over so bad your ass is going to hurt for months." Jackson snarled. Not really at Gladstone, but at memories. The man had definitely been through some big-time pain associated with gambling in the past.

"You might think because they're here that they won't be able to reach you in the States, but they will." He made a wavy motion with his fingers. "They are bacterial scum who will eat away at your life until you have nothing left. Oh, and when all of that isn't enough, they'll go after your family. That little baby and your wife are considered commodities. They'll find out exactly how far you are willing to go for them. I've seen entire families killed for as little as ten thousand dollars. Babies, grandparents, these people don't care. They kill for sport."

There was a long silence.

She started to say something, but Jackson tilted his head toward Gladstone, who appeared tortured. His face contorted into a mass of emotion.

Jackson's words must have finally penetrated the man's skull because his head fell into his hands. "What the hell was I thinking?" he cried out in agony. "She's going to kill me. Oh, God, I don't want to disappoint her again. I'd been doing so well and then the new baby came and we needed to add on to the house." His fist clenched.

"Sales were down at the office and I was worried about my job. I heard about this place from a friend and thought I'd make some quick cash. How could I have been so incredibly stupid?" The last part came out as a groan.

Yep. Mariska didn't say it out loud.

"My only saving grace is that you guys came in before I could borrow any. Though, I'm sorry to say I probably would have. I kept thinking this time it'll be my turn to win. At first I was up almost a hundred thousand."

Jackson cleared his throat to get the man's attention. "I don't know who suggested you come to Bangkok to gamble away your home, but they don't exactly run clean games in a place like that," Jackson said as he wrapped an arm around the headrest. "There are some legitimate clubs operated by the hotels, but not the ones run by these guys.

"Be grateful that we got you out when we did. Go home and make amends. Ask for forgiveness, and get your ass to a meeting."

Gladstone was quiet again.

"You're right," he finally said. "I have to get home. I'm out of control and I've made a royal mess of my life again." He sighed. "Can you guys take me back to the hotel? I can pick up my things and my passport. I want to get the hell out of this place as soon as possible."

"It isn't necessary to take you back to the Four Seasons," Jackson said. "We're taking you straight to the airport. Your bag and papers are in the trunk."

A tiny gasp of surprise escaped Mariska. She couldn't believe he'd done that or had even thought to do it.

He must have read the question on her face. "I thought if we were lucky and did find him tonight, he might need to make a quick exit. I took care of things before we left. It's the Boy Scout in me. I like to be prepared." He winked.

The man was full of surprises. Mar chastised herself for not thinking about what would happen if she did find Gladstone. *Always have an exit strategy.* Whether in a client meeting or when being chased by bad guys, it was one of the things her friend Katie, who used to be a detective with the NYPD, drilled into her.

They pulled up in front of the airport and the driver opened the door nearest Gladstone.

Mariska watched as Jackson jumped out and grabbed Gladstone's bag from the trunk and handed it to him. She pushed the button to roll down the window so she could hear what Jackson said to the other man.

"Go home, Desmond. Tell your wife what you did, then go to a meeting. Those people can help salvage your life. It may feel like it's too late, but it isn't. It may take her a while for her to forgive you, but she will eventually." Jackson stuck out his hand. "Whatever you do, take your ticket and get through security. I can't promise that those guys won't come after you as long as you are still in Thailand. Best if you go as fast as possible."

They shook hands. "Thanks." Gladstone glanced

back at Mariska. "Can you get a message to my wife and let her know I'm on the way? I should do it myself, but I need some time to think. She'll go ballistic no matter what, but I need some time. Um, maybe you could hold off on telling her everything." He sighed. "I'd like to do that myself."

Jackson climbed in the backseat with her.

"He's really messed up," she said. "I can't believe what he's done to his family, he could have put them in mortal danger. How could he think gambling his family's finances away would solve his problems?"

Jackson had a guarded look on his face. "People do crazy things when they're desperate."

Wasn't she going to do something desperate in a few minutes when her courage kicked in? "I guess you're right."

She crossed her hands against her chest to keep from hugging him, which, though she wanted to do it more than anything, was less than professional. "Thank you, Jackson, for your help with this." Mariska suddenly felt awkward. "There's no way I would have found him so quickly if you hadn't helped me."

Jackson gave her one of his devastating smiles and took her hand in his. Mariska's heart pounded an extra beat. "You would have managed fine on your own. You are quite resourceful when you need to be, but it was my pleasure to help," he said as he squeezed her hand gently. "I'm surprised it went as easily as it did. I figured we'd have to hit at least a few more casinos over the next few days before we found him.

"I understand how you feel about Gladstone. The guy needed some tough love. I hope we made it through that stubborn brain of his, but you never know with these guys. They'll say almost anything to get out of a jam."

Mariska noticed that he didn't let go of her fingers, and she didn't bother to mention it. "I sure as hell couldn't have walked up to him like that in the casino. You freaked me out. Can I ask what made you suspect gambling in the first place?"

Jackson frowned for a second. "Instinct, I guess. If it were an affair he'd have no reason to leave the hotel. He's thousands of miles from home, and the Four Seasons is no shack. There are only a few things that keep a man from sleeping for a few days, and gambling is number one on that list."

"Huh. What are some of the others?"

Jackson laughed out loud. "A woman, drinking and there's always death. I prefer the first two myself." He gave her another wink.

Mariska gave a rather unladylike snort. "You crack me up."

Biting her lip, she almost said something about the woman part of his comment, but chickened out. At first she thought she could segue into asking about him joining her in Phuket. She had to give up this craziness. There was no way she would get the courage to ask him.

But her vacation officially started when Gladstone walked into the airport and for once in her life she was ready to have some fun. Jackson made her feel so much more than any man she'd ever met. Even if it was a temporary heat, she needed to burn up in it.

That kiss in the club left her with one thought. *If he's*

that good at kissing, what would the sex be like? The idea of sex with Jackson was the one thing that gave her courage. If he said no, she'd be embarrassed, but she'd survive. Once they left the car, she'd never have to see him again.

Do it.

She was a grown woman with needs. A strong, smart woman who shouldn't feel guilty about going after what she desired. At least that was what she told herself. She'd never asked a guy out, let alone to go away with her on vacation.

Most of her sexual relationships in college were with bored fellow classmen who were as drunk as she was on Saturday night. None of them had come close to Jackson. The way he looked at her sometimes sent her into a spin, twirling so fast she couldn't stop. Crazy girl that she was, she didn't want it to end.

There was also something dark and dangerous about him. Yet, he was compassionate in the way he dealt with Gladstone, knowing exactly what to say to the other man. If she were really honest she had to know more about Jackson. The man was the biggest mystery she'd ever come across, one she desperately wanted to solve.

She took a deep breath. "Uh, I'm heading out to a beach resort and— I, um. This is stupid. Never mind." Mariska couldn't go through with it.

Worry furrowed his brow and he leaned toward her. "What is it? Do you need help with something? I may have some free time in the next couple of days if you have another case, but then I'm traveling again."

You. I need you. She couldn't tell him that.

Now she really felt like an idiot. "Oh, no. Sorry. It has absolutely nothing to do with work." She bit her lip again. "I was wondering if you might like to come with me for a couple of days. I could—" She started to say *pay for his expenses,* which would make him sound like a man whore. This was not going the way she wanted.

Her hands twisted with anxiety. "Sorry. I— You're. Gawd. No. Uh. Never mind. Please forget I said anything. I mean we worked so well together. It's not like any of that was real. The kissing and the way you touched me. Um. Chalk it up to the excitement of the job."

What the hell are you doing?

"I'm so embarrassed. I don't know why I can't shut up. This is one of the most horrifying moments of my life. Well, except when we faced those guards back at the club and there was that time freshman year with the granny panties. See—oh. Gawd. Make me stop." She threw a hand over her mouth. Mortified beyond belief.

Jackson grinned, before glancing out the rear window, then back at her. "Yes, I'll go with you." Taking her left hand from her mouth, he ran his thumb across her fingers and then kissed them.

For a moment she couldn't breathe, and she was fairly certain her body had turned into a puddle of melted butter. Then she wasn't sure if she'd heard him correctly.

Say something.

"Really?"

He chuckled. "Yes. A few days at the beach sounds like a good time to me, especially if I'm with you."

Okay, this time her heart really did stop.

"Wow. Okay. Cool." *Der.* Now she couldn't form sentences. The hunk of gorgeousness across from her wanted to spend the weekend with her. She wouldn't question the gods. She'd be grateful.

Score!

Breathe deep. "When do you want to leave? I thought the case might take a few days, but my reservation is open-ended at the resort from today to the end of the month." There, she sounded quite cosmopolitan, like she had weekend flings all the time.

"Why don't we go tonight? It's the weekend and there's nothing on my agenda that I can't set aside for a few days." Jackson's eyes lingered on her mouth. "I need to run some errands, which will give you time to pack up some of your things. Then we can head out."

Mariska couldn't believe it. In a few hours she'd be alone with Jackson on a remote beach. Her body trembled with need. *Down, girl. We'll be there soon enough.*

7

THE SUN CRESTED THE waves as they pulled up in front of the resort. It had been a long time since Jackson had stopped to watch a sunrise, but he'd promised Mariska so he parked the bike in the small lot to the right of the hotel.

It was more like a large tropical mansion with a few suites for exclusive guests. Several small villas dotted the beach. It was a place where those with money, who valued their privacy, went to relax. The woman had the funds, but he wondered why Mariska had picked it. She didn't seem like someone who liked the solitary life.

Well, she wasn't exactly solitary.

How the hell did I end up at a beach resort with this woman?

What would she expect from him? He was used to lying, but it didn't feel right to do something false with Mariska. Well, any more than he'd already done.

Jackson wasn't one to live with regrets or guilt, but he didn't like using her.

If it keeps you alive it'll be worth it.

It wasn't that he didn't want her.

That's the problem. I want her too much. And she's too damn good for the likes of me. The last thing she needs is some renegade spook putting her life in danger.

He should deposit her in her room, and make an excuse that he had business back in the city. He'd accidentally keep her computer and send it to her when he heard from Dawson. Honestly, he had no idea why his handler had arranged for them to meet. The more he had come to know Mariska, the less the dots connected.

They stood on the beach watching the horizon. The waves lapping against the shore were the only sound, and it was the most peaceful moment Jackson had experienced in years. He forced himself to concentrate on the scene before him and let his mind rest for a few seconds. He could figure out his next move later.

"Is it me or does the sun seem even bigger here." Her voice was soft as a feather and full of awe. She leaned back against his chest. It seemed such a natural move, like they'd been together for years. Automatically, he wrapped his arms around her.

After all, the woman deserved some comfort after what they'd been through. She was a trouper, this one, and hadn't complained about the zigzag path he tore through Bangkok to lose the tail they'd picked up while trying to leave the hotel. The dark black sedan that had followed them at the airport had been waiting outside the garage. Knowing it might be a possibility, Jackson had planned ahead, and lost the car about three minutes into the chase. Then after he was sure they were safe, he'd backtracked to make sure the casino thugs thought they'd gone the opposite direction.

Mariska had held tight to him, never saying a word, though he did feel her hands fist with nerves a few times. Hell, if he hadn't been gripping the handlebar of the Japanese motorcycle he might have been doing the same thing. If he told her to lean right or left she did, never questioning his instincts.

He was surprised that she didn't begin her nervous chattering as soon as they were free of the nuisance. He figured she needed to process the fact that they'd been so close to danger. The more he was around her the more he realized she wasn't used to being in the middle of the action.

"The sun does seem larger," he said. "Of course that probably has something to do with a serious lack of pollution, which can dull—"

She slapped at the arm he'd wrapped around her waist. "Don't ruin it for me with facts, let me have the magic."

He grinned. She was definitely a woman who deserved some magic.

He already knew about her mother, but more research revealed that she'd taken over her mother's agency right out of college. She had finished her Ph.D. in clinical psychology with an emphasis on the criminal mind.

That explained why textbook-wise she seemed like a smart investigator, but she didn't have many practical skills.

The confidence he'd seen earlier had been an act. He knew that now and it made him like her even more. She did whatever it took to get the job done. That was something they had in common. She also had good natural instincts. At the club and the massage parlor she'd acted the parts as if she'd been born to them.

She needed to work on watching the world around her. Maybe he could teach her to be more observant before they had to part ways.

There he went again, acting like he might hang around.

He sighed, and she turned to him.

"Are you sorry you came with me? I can be a bit of a romantic at times. I'm not expecting anything from you." She frowned. "I mean. You know I think we can be friends."

"Friends?" He smiled at her. "Yes, that's a possibility. But I can tell you that I'm expecting a great deal from you." He kissed her again. He couldn't seem to stop himself from doing that, and wondered if her lipstick had some kind of pheromone that drew him to her full lips. He'd seen stranger things in his business. "Finished with your sunrise?"

She gave a happy sigh, and smiled back at him. That small gesture sent warmth through his body. His cock stirred and he pulled away before she could feel his physical interest. "Maybe we should check in."

Taking her hand, he started up the beach, but she stopped him. "About that. I—rented one of the villas on the beach. And there's only—um. There's only one bed. I can try and change it. They may have a suite where you could have your own room?"

Two rooms wasn't a bad idea. He already felt unsure about advancing their friendship without being completely honest with her. And frankly, he wasn't sure how long he'd be able to withstand her charms, since he desired her more than anyone he'd ever met. It scared the hell out of him.

"Oh. Wow." Her voice rose in pitch, her face pinched in distress. "That silence answered my question loud and clear. Now I'm really embarrassed. I'll see if I can get the suite."

His nonanswer had been misinterpreted. This time he was the one who stopped her from walking. Taking her in his arms, he pressed his lips against hers. Sweet. She tasted so sweet and warm. He'd first noticed it when their lips met at the club, and now that same sensation sent his mind in a million different directions, eventually landing in one thought.

He wanted to take her right there on the beach.

Finally he lifted his face from hers. "We can go as fast or as slow as you want. You don't strike me as a woman who likes to rush into things, but have no doubt that I desire you, Mariska Stonegate." He meant every word.

Part of his brain screamed he was an ass for getting involved with her. He'd only break her heart in a few days, and there was always that looming possibility of getting them both killed if Vlad caught up with them.

The other part of his brain said, "Screw it." Jackson wasn't sure he'd leave Thailand alive. Burned CIA agents didn't have long retirements. Whatever his future held, he had to spend the next few days with this woman.

It probably wasn't fair to either of them, but at least he'd have memories of her. And he would do his best to make sure she had the time of her life.

"So, you've figured out I've never done anything

like this before." She scrunched up her face. She was so adorable.

"If it makes you feel any better I can honestly say I've never run off on a beach vacation with a woman." Well, at least when it wasn't for work. He'd done it in the line of duty, but there'd never been time for any relationships. He'd become a machine the last six years. Everything was about the job.

Now they didn't give a crap about him.

But Mariska did. That she desired him as much as he did her was enough. A few days on a beach wouldn't be much of a hardship. He'd give her that, knowing he was the one receiving the real gift.

Taking her hand in his, he led her up to the lobby of the hotel.

"Okay, so we have one of the water villas right on the beach. We're going to have fab views, I'm told. At least I think that's what the desk clerk said." She smiled at him, covering her discomfort. "I think he's French, and his English was almost so perfect I couldn't understand him."

"Mar, don't be nervous around me. The villa is great," he assured her. "I'll keep my promise. We'll take our time. We both need to relax and have some fun. There's nothing wrong with that."

It might kill him to take it slow. This woman made him burn like no other, but it wouldn't be such a bad way to die. He'd almost been killed in a myriad of ways. Yes, he much preferred dying from pining after a woman he didn't deserve, as long as he could do it in her presence.

When she reached up and kissed his cheek it

surprised him. "That's the problem. I don't want to go slow, Jackson." With that she took his hand and all but dragged him to their small villa.

This is going to be one hell of a ride. Jackson followed her like a smitten puppy.

8

I'm about to sleep with Jackson. Okay, lungs, breathe.

The short trip down the beach path to the villa seemed to take forever. Mariska had never thought of herself as particularly bold, but it was as if a sexy alien had taken over her body. Jackson caused her to say and do things she'd only fantasized about.

The last year had been about her pretending to be something she wasn't. Everyone thought because she was Janice Stonegate's daughter she could step right into her mother's shoes. But those shoes had been about two sizes too big and Mariska constantly played catch-up. Hiding the fact that she lacked the basic skills to be a decent investigator had worn her out.

When she went back to the office she'd tell the rest of the staff the truth. They deserved it. Though she would still meet with clients. That was something she was good at. Discerning the needs of whoever walked in the door.

But she couldn't think about all of that now. Here at the beach was a time to let go and be herself—maybe for the first time in a long time. Maybe for the first time ever.

There'd been a moment on the beach when she'd almost died of embarrassment. Thinking she'd assumed too much, but Jackson pushed all those fears away with a heart-dropping kiss and his tender words. She wondered if he had any idea how into him she was.

It'd probably scare the hell out of him if he did.

They hadn't discussed the harrowing ride from Bangkok to Phuket, but it had taken everything she had not to throw up on the back of that bike. Several times she closed her eyes and listened to Jackson bark orders as he took a fast corner, or needed her to lean a certain way.

It had been one of the scariest moments of her life, but also the most thrilling. Now they were here, and she wanted to leave everything in the past behind. To live for the now—that was the promise she'd made to herself.

Sliding the key card into the door of the villa, Jackson opened it and they both stood at the entrance taking it all in. The space was deceptively larger than it appeared from the outside.

Everything was white, from the filmy curtains and the bedspread to the walls. The French doors could be pushed to the side, opening the whole front of the place to the ocean breezes and amazing views. She finally walked across the room and peeked around the corner to find a well-appointed bathroom. There was a shower for two, a sink and toilet.

There was also a row of cabinets, a wet bar with shelves of snacks and booze. Mariska realized she was suddenly very hungry. She'd also lost some of the bravado from a few seconds ago.

Is it a bad thing to have a mai tai for breakfast?

It all seemed too real. She was at a beachfront resort with a hot guy who wanted her. He'd even used the word *desire* out on the beach. She should pounce on him, but she needed a little time to pull herself together.

"I know you have to be as exhausted as I am, but how about some breakfast on the beach?" She picked up the menu by the bed. "I'm starving."

"Great idea." Jackson put their bags down inside the armoire. "Do they have pancakes, and maybe some bacon? I could use some protein."

"You're my kind of man." *In more ways than one.* "A full breakfast it is." She picked up the phone and ordered, adding a mai tai at the end. The room service staff agreed to set the food up on the patio table right outside their door.

"How about we take a quick swim to work out the kinks?" Jackson smiled at her, and her pulse quickened. After what she'd seen at the massage parlor, she couldn't wait for another chance to see him sans clothes. The man's body begged to be touched, and she planned to do that a lot.

Suddenly tongue-tied, she coughed into her hand. "Uh, great idea." She reached into her bag and scooped out one of the four bikinis she'd thrown in. This one was red with tiny bows on each side. It was one of her favorites. "Five minutes. I'll meet you out on the beach."

She heard him chuckle as she shut the door.

Mariska stared at herself in the mirror.

Live for the now.

She'd seen the phrase on a fortune cookie a month ago. It was the cookie that had inspired the trip to Thailand. Tired of living in the past and worrying about what everyone else thought of her, she'd decided it was time for a real vacation. One where she could be whomever she wanted, and maybe she'd find herself.

Mariska grabbed the side of the sink.

"You better watch out, Jackson. I'm a bold woman who isn't going to shy away from life anymore. I'm going to have my way with you. Mmm, in every which way I can. I'm done with boundaries. It's all about being in the now and living life to the fullest."

OUTSIDE THE VILLA, Jackson did a quick search of the perimeter. He'd lost the tail before they even left the city, but he couldn't be too careful. If someone had seen him with Mariska, it wouldn't be hard to track her down since she'd probably used her credit card to book the hotel.

He'd been surprised when she didn't jump his bones the minute they walked in the door. From the slight quiver in her voice, it sounded as if she'd contracted another case of the nerves.

She might be a woman of contradictions, but he didn't care. Life would never be boring around her, and he liked that he couldn't always read her.

He'd meant what he told her earlier about going at her pace. To him, she was a delicacy. One he intended to savor. He could wait.

As he watched Mariska walk down the beach, Jackson was glad he'd already jumped into a cool wave.

The water hid his instant erection. The woman had no idea the kind of effect she had on him. The second he saw her in that damn red bikini he swore he'd send a thank-you letter to the designer. It fit her body perfectly. Her pert breasts were covered barely enough to make the mind wonder how long it would take to untie that little bow between them, and the ones on the sides of her beautiful, curvy hips.

As she moved closer to him the cool water slapped against her taut belly, and her nipples hardened into tiny buds pressing against the material. Using her right hand, she shaded her eyes from the sun. "You started without me."

You have no idea. Jackson reached out to her, careful to stay waist deep so she couldn't see the tent in his board shorts, at least not yet. "The water was too enticing. Of course I could say the same about that bikini."

As she reached him, he saw the blush on her cheeks. "Do you have any idea how beautiful you are?"

She ducked her head and stared down at the water. "Um, are there sharks here? I really don't like sharks."

Jackson laughed hard at that. "You're nervous again."

"No, no." She waved her hand. "I'm kind of a freak about sharks. Well, sharks and snakes. Probably too much Discovery Channel as a child. Great whites like cold water, right?"

She was hot and cold, this one. But he was a patient man.

"There are about seventeen different species in this

part of the world, including the nurse, whale and tiger sharks, but most of them prefer the deeper waters, so I think we're okay. How good of a swimmer are you?"

She bit her lip but finally met his eyes. "I'm pretty good. Why? Do you think we'll have to outswim the sharks? I'd rather sit on the sand if that's the case. That is exactly why I like surfing. At least you have something to climb on to if you see a fin."

Jackson couldn't keep from chuckling again. "I had no idea you surfed. We'll have to do that while we're here. I thought maybe we could swim out to that deck a little to the right." He pointed over his shoulder. "But we can stay right here with our feet on the ocean floor, if it makes you feel better."

She glanced down at the water again, right at his erection. As she moved closer, something came over her face. It took him a moment to realize it was lust.

"What do you want to do, Jackson?" Her voice had turned velvety again, and so suggestive that all of his senses went on alert. He didn't think it was a possibility, but his cock grew even harder.

Not bothering to answer, he took her hands in his and brought her slick body against him. She smelled sweet and salty and he had to taste her. Sliding his arms around her waist, he pulled her with him farther into the water, where their bodies were hidden but he could still keep his feet firm on the sandy bottom.

They stared at each other for a moment. The need he saw there was something he wanted to vanquish.

Mar leaned into him and captured his lips. That's all it took. His determination to take things slowly swam away with the fish.

I want her.

Trailing kisses down her neck, he moved to her shoulder, and back to her lips, assaulting them. When she responded with equal passion, he brought her even closer.

She smiled against his lips, and pushed her pelvis into his. "You have a revolver in there, or are you happy to see me?"

Jackson nipped at her ear. "Guns and water don't mix, so use your imagination."

"Oh, I'd say you have a loaded gun ready to go." Then she touched him there, and he almost exploded in her hand. Another second and he might.

Jackson watched her face as she traced the length of him, and he knew she wanted him as much as he did her. But he had to stop her hand before he embarrassed himself.

Turning Mariska so that her back was to him, he slid his hand beneath one of the triangles and lightly pinched one of her nipples.

"Mmm." She moaned and it was one of the sexiest sounds he'd ever heard. Pleasing her was the only thing on his mind. He'd do anything to hear that sound again.

As he moved his hand over her breast, his other one slid down lower to the triangle of cloth between her legs. The first touch in the folds of softness sent her body pressing into his.

Her arms snaked up behind her and around his neck so she could balance. She rocked herself against his erection as he found the tiny nub that drove her to move faster and faster against him. Her soft bottom coaxed his erection into a frenzy. Using his forefinger he rubbed, alternately sliding a finger into her.

"Jackson," she whispered, but she didn't stop moving her softness against his hard cock. He felt the tension build in her. "Mmm," she said again and he intensified the motion of his fingers. "Oh, my—" A low groan came from deep within her, and then a shuddering release. Her body relaxed and he had a feeling she would have slid into the ocean had she not been holding on to his neck.

She was languid in his arms, but his body was tense and aching for release. Turning so that she faced him, she pulled him toward her and kissed him hard. Sliding one of her hands down, she began pumping his swollen cock.

"Mar," he growled and deepened their kiss.

"Did you see how fast you made me come? Do the same thing. Come for me, baby," she whispered against his lips. The friction of her hand, along with the slickness of the seawater, sent Jackson reeling. It wasn't long before his cock exploded with a force that almost knocked him off his feet and into the depths of the ocean.

Taking a cleansing breath, he steadied them both and kissed her again. Teasing her with his tongue and relishing the taste of her.

Mar wrapped her legs around him. "I'm a pirate, and I've captured you. I thought you should know," she warned him.

He smiled and nipped at her ear. "Are you going to keep me in your quarters and have your way with me?"

"Oh, yes." Her voice had dipped low again as her

finger teased his neck. "I'm going to keep you naked and make you pleasure me over and over again. I'll only allow you to stop for the occasional meal, and maybe a few hours' rest. I'm insatiable, you know. I'm going to wear you out in a big way."

Jackson couldn't keep from laughing. "I see. Well, I guess I'm resigned to my fate. Do with me what you wish, fair maiden."

She lifted an eyebrow.

"I mean, very scary pirate woman." He corrected himself and tried to give her a serious look, which failed miserably.

Mar moved her body against his crotch. "Oh, I will do exactly what I wish, don't worry about that."

Jackson decided right then that he very much liked being a pirate woman's booty call.

9

SOMETHING PRICKED HIS SENSES, and Jackson reluctantly pulled his mouth from Mar's. Still in the water, he scanned the area, searching for the intrusion. Even with the distraction of the woman wrapped around him, his training always kicked in.

There was movement outside their villa and his eyes narrowed.

He relaxed when he realized their breakfast had arrived. A waiter dressed in a white coat and black pants had set the table.

"Time to eat," he whispered in her ear.

"Um, suddenly I'm not so hungry for food." She gave him a saucy wink.

He kissed her neck. "Trust me, you're going to need tons of protein. I have such plans for you."

He delighted in her soft laugh as she pushed away from him. Jackson straightened and was surprised that his cock was already missing her touch. The back side of her provided one luscious view as she bounced on to the beach.

Yes, he'd feed her and then he was going to make

love to her on a bed where he could see her face as he drove into her. His mission for the next twenty-four hours was to make her scream with pleasure as many times as possible.

It's a tough task, but I'm ready for the challenge.

After running on to the beach, he grabbed a towel. A king's feast had been set up on a teak table. Fruit, pancakes, bacon, eggs, muffins and toast.

Mariska was already biting into a strawberry. She looked so carefree, wrapped in a towel and sitting cross-legged in her chair. She'd pulled her long hair into a clip and even with no makeup she was a stunner.

She caught him staring and brought a napkin to her chin to wipe her red and oh-so-kissable lips. "Do I have juice on my face? I can't help it. This fruit is so fresh. It's been so long since I've had a meal, I feel like I could eat everything here."

Jackson wrapped his towel around his waist and sat down. Stabbing a fork into a couple of pancakes, he put them on his plate. "Hope you don't mind if I take a couple of these before you inhale the rest." He grinned at her, taking the bite out of his words.

The smile she gave him made his heart do funny things. "Probably a good idea," she said. "I happen to be a pancake freak. In college those poor waitresses at IHOP cringed when I came in to study on Endless Pancake Day. You have to try the bacon. It's from heaven. I don't know why I love fried pig so much, but I do."

This time he was the one who laughed. "Fried pig?"

She shrugged. "We couldn't say the word *bacon* in our house. We had this old retriever, Terry the Terrible, who would knock you down if you said it. The dog loved him some bacon. While his ears were great, his sense of smell wasn't. If you called it fried pig you could usually make it to the table with the plate."

Jackson leaned forward. "You had a dog named Terry the Terrible?"

Rolling her eyes, she set down her fork. "You have no idea. He was an awful dog to everyone but the family. He was my grand protector. When people came over I had to keep him in the backyard or he'd sit and growl at them the whole time. He never bit anyone but he'd bark and make this low guttural sound, and basically scare the heck out of them."

Jackson enjoyed listening to her talk. He could imagine a mean old dog determined to protect her. Hell, he'd known her less than a day, and he wanted to take care of her, even though she seemed perfectly capable of doing that for herself.

"My mom and dad traveled a lot when I was little, and Terry was my best friend." She snorted. "Now, that sounds pathetic—a dog as a best friend. Bring out the violins. Did you have pets?" she asked as she poured syrup on her pancakes.

Jackson considered his answer. There was the one time that he had tried to hide a kitten. When his mom's boyfriend found it he'd gone ballistic, and had beaten Jackson for ten minutes with a belt. Screaming that the last thing they needed was another mouth to feed.

The next day Jackson rode the bus two hours to the shelter and then begged the woman at the desk to promise she'd find a good home for the kitten.

A week later he went back to check to make sure the

animal had been adopted and not killed. The woman at the desk had taken pity on him and explained that a nice family had taken in the animal and named him Hal. She promised that the family loved the kitten very much. She even showed him the file with a picture of the family with the kitten so he could see she told the truth.

Sitting on the back of the bus, he cried all the way home. He was seven, and after that he made it a point to never care too much about anything. "No. I never had pets. We moved too much."

He never liked discussing himself, especially anything to do with the past, and decided to steer the conversation in a new direction.

"How long have you had your investigative agency?" Jackson knew the answer, but it was the first thing that came to his mind.

"Wow. Um, it's been about eighteen months, I guess." Her voice faltered for an instant. "My mom was killed in a plane crash, and she willed the place to me. They do a lot of good work there, from finding missing children to consulting with law enforcement agencies around the world. They make a difference, and I planned to be a part of it some day. I never expected it to happen so soon."

"That must have been rough on you with your mom. I'm sorry."

She sighed. "I'm not sure I'll ever be up to her standards. She was incredible at what she did. People tell me her instincts were legendary. I didn't spend much time with her when I was a kid, but in my teen years. Well, she made sure I could protect myself, and made me take martial arts even if I'd rather be practicing with makeup. I'm grateful now. But at the time, all we did was fight. When I went away to college most of our communication was through my dad. It's always been easier for me to connect with him. I'd always planned on getting to know my mom better, and then the crash."

She adjusted the ponytail on top of her head, and rolled her shoulders as if to loosen tension that had built there. "Can I tell you a secret?"

Jackson was intrigued. "Of course, you can tell me anything."

Staring down at the table, she twisted the napkin in her hand. He had a hard time reading her face and was more curious than ever.

"Whatever it is, Mar, really," he encouraged her.

"This case, in Bangkok, was my first one. Well, technically, that is. I solved one in Texas, but that was a complete accident. Something I happened to walk in on, but this was my first one to actually take on and solve." She pointed at him. "With your help, of course. I really don't think I could have done it without you."

His assumption from his earlier reading was correct. While she seemed to have some of the basics down, that she'd missed the tail and hadn't caught on that he wasn't who he said he was had clued him in.

"Really?" He pretended surprise. "Huh. You're pretty good for a newbie, and I bet you would have found him on your own. Though, you might have taken a different approach."

This time her grin went from one side of her face to the other, and he knew he'd said the right thing.

"Thank you. One thing is for sure, I would have

never thought to go to a massage parlor to get intel." She laughed.

"Well, none of us is perfect, and to be honest, I was following what little trail we had on him," Jackson told her. "The best way to find people is usually to retrace their steps. That's all we did. When you're investigating it's about following the clues you have and using those to your advantage. I could help you, you know?"

"What?" She folded her napkin and put it on the table.

"Well, the only time you really slipped up was after we dropped Gladstone off at the airport. We picked up a tail. Were you aware of that?"

Her brow furrowed. "I had no idea. That's why you drove pretty crazy on the bike."

"Right." Jackson leaned back in the chair. "When you're on a case you have to be hyperaware of your surroundings. I've noticed you're good at reading people, but you lack the basics in observation techniques. I tell you what, let's practice right now. Look straight at me, and tell me what you've observed on the beach since we've been sitting here."

She bit her lip again, but did as he said. "I can hear someone talking, but it seems really far away. Um, and the waves are really loud. That's about it."

He hadn't lied. This was something he could teach her in the little time they had together.

"Okay, now look around."

She did as he asked.

"To your right there's a couple about a hundred yards down the beach. She's wearing a dark blue bikini. His suit is yellow. The man does not have the physique to wear a banana hammock, but there you go."

"And he's kind of furry. Ick," she added and then laughed.

He grinned at her. "They have a basket of muffins and juice," Jackson continued. "She's mad at him because he passed out from drinking too much last night. He's ignoring her.

"Beyond them to the right, there's a bodyguard hidden in the trees. He's watching the couple, and he's carrying a gun on his right hip. You can tell that by the way he stands. He's wearing a white shirt over the top of khakis trying to blend in as a tourist, but he's not. He doesn't fit into the crowd that stays here, and it's apparent by the scowl on his face."

Glancing around, Mariska held up a hand. "This is kind of freaky, Jackson. Your back is to all of them. How could you possibly know that?"

"I've had years of training. But I always stay aware of my surroundings."

She stood. "You have to teach me that. I mean it, that's friggin' incredible what you did."

"It's a matter of learning to see between the lines and paying attention at all times. It's hard work at first, but soon it will become second nature. First you focus on the people and memorize what they're wearing, approximate height, and anything that might help you distinguish them in a crowd."

"You amaze me. How long have you been a detective?" she asked.

Damn. Caught. The first thing an operative learned was to stick as close to the truth as possible. "I've been in the business, one way or another, for about eight years, but not always as a detective. I did some time in the military."

Close enough.

He steered the conversation back to safer territory. "While we're here, we'll work on some of the basics. You'll begin to feel more comfortable. You've got good instincts, so you're well on your way."

Mar leaned over and kissed the top of his head. "You're such a sweet man. I don't know about my instincts, but I definitely appreciate the help."

After spreading her towel down on the large two-person lounger, she sat down on the right side of it and brushed the sand from her feet. "I think my eyes were way bigger than my stomach. I shouldn't have eaten that fifth pancake. I'm going to finish drying off and start on my tan." She laughed.

Jackson followed her actions and stretched out beside her. After a few seconds he sat up, and reached over and kissed her long and hard.

"Mmm," she said against his lips. "I'm so glad you're here with me."

Jackson stretched out again. "Me, too." He meant it. Though he still worried that spending time together wasn't the best idea for either of them, he couldn't bring himself to leave.

Besides, the pirate wench had captured his heart, and he wasn't quite ready to leave it with her yet.

10

Mariska sat straight up in bed, panicked in the unfamiliar surroundings. It took her a few seconds to remember she was in the villa at the resort. Only a tiny bit of light filtered through the filmy curtains. The room was dark otherwise.

Jackson wasn't in the bed with her, and uneasiness skittered across her skin. "Jackson?" He didn't answer. She listened for the running water, but he wasn't in the shower. She fumbled on the side table until she found a lamp. Blinking a few times, her eyes eventually focused. She glanced down to see she was still in her bikini.

Sliding her feet off the side, she went in search of the man. There was a small desk in the corner where she found a note.

Checking out the grounds and amenities. Will be back in time for dinner. I made reservations at the restaurant for nine to give you time to rest. There's also a snack for you inside the fridge.

"I love that he always thinks of everything." Mariska smiled and stretched. Her skin was tight and smelled like the ocean. She must have passed out on the lounger and Jackson put her to bed. The jet lag and their adventures the last twenty-four hours had finally caught up with her.

"Idiot. You wasted a whole afternoon sleeping." She chided herself. Recalling their time in the water, her body shivered with pleasure. There were so many things she wanted to do with him, and to him.

Remembering how his hand had slipped over her nipple, her body tingled. She gave a happy sigh. She'd never come so fast in her life as she did in that ocean. Knowing she could bring him to orgasm equally as fast made her feel powerful.

At the time she thought it funny that they could be so passionate and then be friendly sitting on the beach eating breakfast. In some ways he seemed so dark and mysterious, and in others he was accessible and kind.

As good as she was at reading people, she never could quite get a fix on him. The man was restless, and she could tell he never stayed in one place too long, which meant the most she could expect out of him was a couple of days. Something told her that he'd been more worried about those men being after him than her. That meant he might be in some kind of trouble.

They might part ways soon but that made her even more determined to make the hours, and if she was lucky, days, she had with him memorable.

A small grumble in her stomach sent her to the fridge where she found a tiny bottle of champagne and some chocolate-covered strawberries. The man absolutely nailed the way to her heart. Popping the cork on the champagne, she filled one of the glasses he left on the counter. Biting down on the strawberry, she savored the mix of chocolate sweetness and the tart juice as they slid across her tongue.

Finding her watch in her bag, she saw that it was nearing seven. That gave her plenty of time to get ready.

Jackson's bag was under the counter near the fridge and she was tempted to snoop. Her nosy disposition was the one thing she had inherited from her mother. As she was about to reach down, she made herself stop; whatever she found wouldn't change how she felt about him. And how much did she really need to know other than he was gorgeous and seemed intent on pleasing her?

Nothing.

Maybe he was dangerous, but he wouldn't hurt her—at least physically. Emotionally, she wasn't so sure. Their short time together already left her with a craving for the man's kisses.

"You knew going into this that it was short-term, so don't go getting any crazy ideas." She said the words out loud as if that would make her more accepting of the statement.

While he might think she wasn't the most perceptive woman in the world, she had deduced he was much more than a detective who traveled the world on cases. He'd mentioned the military and he had that air about him. Then there were the scars. She'd noticed the bullet wounds on his shoulder and back. There was what seemed like a knife wound near his heart, and he had a multitude of scars on his thighs.

Yes, he'd most definitely led a dangerous life, but he had only treated her with kindness. Normally, Mariska didn't go for the protective type, but she liked that he wanted to take care of her. And she honestly wanted to take care of him.

Every time she asked about his past, a haunted look came over his face. More than anything she wanted to clear away those cobwebs of sadness. She'd noticed it when he talked to Gladstone about his father, and then again when she'd mentioned the pets.

She wouldn't make the mistake of delving back into his childhood. He masked the pain well, but she could tell the memories hurt.

She felt a sort of compulsion to make him happy. They had such a wonderful chemistry, a connection she wasn't sure she'd ever experienced with another man. She wondered—

Be a big girl and don't let those fantasies of happily ever after get in the way. Live in the now. There's nothing wrong with having fun and allowing yourself the freedom to enjoy life with a sexy man for a few days.

After eating the berries and taking a few sips of the champagne, she ventured into the bathroom. It smelled of Jackson. Warm and sensual with a hint of amber and sandalwood, the mere scent of him made her pelvis tighten with need.

Catching sight of herself in the mirror, she let out a yelp. "Thank God he isn't here to see me." Her hair had fallen out of its ponytail and stuck straight out from her head. Luckily Jackson must have carried her in before she had too much sun. While her skin was dry, she hadn't turned pink.

The steamy shower helped to wash away her sleepy mind and brought her back to being human. The hotel had provided an array of soaps and lotions and she used the freesia-scented shampoo and conditioner. Once she finished, she lathered her skin with the same scented lotion. She felt like an exotic flower when she walked out of the bathroom.

Leaving the towel wrapped around her, she went in search of her clothes. Her large backpack had been emptied and she found Jackson had hung up her sarongs along with her jeans and T-shirts, and he'd carefully placed everything else in drawers at the bottom of the armoire. It didn't bother her that he'd gone through her things, because she could tell he'd taken special care in making sure everything was done right. He'd also saved her some ironing.

Mariska was grateful she'd only picked her sexiest lingerie to make the trip. That's when it dawned on her. She had meant to buy condoms at the hotel in Bangkok, but didn't have time.

"Crap. I hope the gift shop is still open." She'd noticed the small alcove with sundry items when she'd checked them into the hotel. *Surely they have some.* At least she hoped so. After their bit of fun in the ocean, making love to the man had become a priority for Mar.

Dressing quickly, she threw on a touch of makeup. She intended to dash to the hotel and back before Jackson returned from his walk.

Using the path they'd taken to get down to the villa, she scrambled her way up the slight hill to the hotel.

Luckily the little store was open. The condoms came in small boxes of six.

Mar stood there contemplating, her fingers tapping on her chin.

I have no idea what to do? How long will he be here? Will I look like a vacation ho if I buy all of the stock?

After chewing on her nail for a minute, she bought five boxes.

To his credit, the elderly clerk didn't even show the slightest hint of merriment that the crazy American was buying his place out of condoms. Mariska tried not to be mortified. She was a grown woman, for goodness' sake. Still, she'd never purchased quite so many. After she'd signed the ticket to charge everything to her room the clerk put the items in a discreet bag along with some sunscreen she needed.

Before leaving the lobby she glanced into the restaurant. She hadn't brought anything dressy to wear, and was relieved to see that though the surroundings were beautiful and formal with linens and crystal, everyone dressed casually.

As she stepped out of the lobby onto the beachfront she noticed the sun as it sank deep into the ocean. She couldn't have picked a more magical place to rest and relax. That she had a gorgeous, if somewhat mysterious, man with her was one big, handsome bonus.

Thinking of him, she hurried down the path.

"Going somewhere?" A voice came out of the shadow of the trees.

Mariska squeaked and dropped her bag.

Jackson stepped out from behind the trees lining the path. "We really do need to practice you being more aware of your surroundings." He bent down to pick up the bag and the few things that had fallen out, including three of the five boxes of condoms.

Mariska looked away.

Jackson put the items back in the bag without commenting on her purchases. "You're beautiful, by the way."

The comment took her so off guard Mariska didn't know what to say. "Thanks," she finally whispered.

The man was beyond awesome when it came to manners. One of the many reasons she adored him. That list grew by the minute.

He leaned down and sniffed her neck and hair, leaving small kisses as he did. The sensual moment sent instant heat between Mariska's legs.

"Maybe we should skip dinner in the restaurant and order room service." Jackson moved his mouth to her lips.

"I think that's a really great idea," she whispered, her voice hot with need.

A horrible gurgling sound came from her stomach.

Jackson stifled a laugh.

"That was so not glamorous or romantic," she said, mortified.

"I think I'm going to have to feed you first, after all." Jackson kissed her again. "But I still like the room service idea."

As soon as they hit the villa door, Jackson had a plan in mind that called for some wine, steak and shrimp. They'd both need the protein for the long haul. A large salad and every dessert on the menu finished off the room service order.

There was a slightly awkward moment when he hung up the phone. She stared at him strangely. He'd been worried when he checked the room and found her gone. Racing up to the hotel, he'd stopped himself when he caught a glimpse of her in the gift store.

He'd delighted in the look of concentration on her face as she tried to figure out how many condoms they'd need. He didn't have the heart to tell her that he'd taken care of that problem earlier in the day.

"You must have a really big sweet tooth." She teased him about ordering so many desserts.

He walked across the room and held her hands in his. "I do." If she only knew she was the real dessert. "Let's go walk on the beach."

The surprise on her face amused him. She'd obviously thought they would make love immediately, but once they began tonight he had no plans of stopping.

Confusion drew her brows together.

"There's something I want to show you," he said as a way of explaining. Then waggled an eyebrow at her. "Did you think I would pounce on you as soon as we made it into the room?"

She gave him a sly grin. "I kind of hoped so, but you're right. Food is always a good thing, and a walk on the beach is—kind of sweet. I had no idea you were such a romantic. The champagne, strawberries and now a walk on the beach."

Oh, you have no idea. Jackson took her hand and led her out the door.

"Wow, the moon's as big as the sun was earlier, but

much easier to look at. And don't start talking to me about the pollution." She laughed softly.

The glow of the orb turned the ocean a silvery black. Jackson squeezed her hand. "I wouldn't dare. Now, listen carefully." They stood at the edge of the water.

It took her a minute, but then he knew she heard it. "That's beautiful, what kind of bird is it?"

"A robin, and it only sings at night. You hear it as the moon comes up and then it stops. Can you see it there a little to the left in those palm trees?"

Mariska gave a tiny gasp. "It has a red breast like the ones at home, but what's that weird thing on its head?"

"That tuft of yellow feathers is what attracts the females, well, that and his call. The bigger the feathers, the more endowed he is." The bird flew away, his song complete for the night.

"Wow. I bet he has some pretty happy lady friends, because those are some big feathers," Mar said.

Jackson guffawed as he put his arm around her shoulders. "You are funny."

"You must have a special interest in this stuff," she said.

Jackson hugged her. "I read a lot as a kid. I thought at one time I might be a scientist of some sort, maybe a biologist or an oceanographer. That's how I knew about the sharks this morning. I read everything about animals and creatures I could when I was a kid. I was absolutely fascinated by them."

Jackson surprised himself by how easily he shared his previous life with her. Usually anything to do with his past was off-limits, but she was so easy to talk to.

Standing on the beach with this woman, he opened up to her more than he had in years. Oh, he knew it wasn't much, but it was a lot more than he'd given anyone else.

These memories weren't painful like those from this morning. The books about the animals kept him in school. When he graduated he planned to go to college and study to be a scientist, but he needed money. That's when he joined the army, and his life went in a much different direction.

"I really love animals, too, except for reptiles and sharks. When I was seven, I decided I had to have a horse," Mar said wistfully. "I was consumed by the prospect of galloping around on daily rides, and braiding its mane and tail." She rolled her eyes. "I blame it on those crazy My Little Pony toys.

"We lived most of the time in Austin, but my mom was an investigator and traveled a lot. Dad had his company but he let me travel with him in the summer. Me and Layla."

"Layla?"

"She was part nanny and part tutor, and she became a dear friend. She lives in Florida now with her family, but she took great care of me when I was a kid." She waved a hand. "I digress.

"My dad could tell I wouldn't let the horse thing go, so he sent me to a dude ranch for three weeks that summer. He thought the hard work would turn me off. It did at first. The 5:00 a.m. wake ups and shoveling horse manure in the barns wasn't my idea of a five-star vacation—even back then I liked to be comfortable when I traveled."

"There's nothing wrong with that." Jackson waved a hand toward the villa. "Some people like to be pampered, some like adventures. To each his own." Not that he'd ever been on a real vacation, but he'd thought about it a lot the last few years. Funny that those thoughts actually had been about a beach with a beautiful woman and crazy umbrella drinks.

"True." She pushed her hair behind her ears. "I eventually fell in love with those horses. Funny thing is, my dad's plan worked, but not in the way he expected.

"After caring for the animals I realized it wouldn't be fair to a horse because I wouldn't be able to ride every day, and we didn't have stables close to the house so someone would have to drive me to wherever we boarded him. I'd already named him Wind." She snorted. "That's such a dumb name, even for a fictional horse. It wasn't practical and I knew that. I cried when I left that ranch, even though I was beat up and bruised from all the work.

"My dad was surprised when I told him that I didn't want a horse after all, and I explained why. I was so practical about it all, that my dad bought me a puppy. Enter Terry the Terrible."

Jackson squeezed her tighter. "That name still cracks me up."

"At first he traveled with us, but he hated it. That's when I decided to stay home with Layla, and began going to a real school." She stepped away from him. "There I go again telling my life story."

"I like hearing about your past," Jackson told her and he meant it. "I want to hear more, but it sounds like the food is on the way." He'd heard the table rolling down the hill a few seconds ago.

She turned around to watch as the waiter moved everything into their villa. "How do you do that? I saw him rolling that cart and I still didn't hear it. Maybe I need to get my hearing checked."

He kissed her ear and nibbled at the lobe. "Your ears are exquisite."

She giggled. "I'm serious. Really, you have to teach me how you do that. On the beach this morning, I could hear those people talking but no way could I concentrate enough to understand the conversation."

"I promise I will impart as much wisdom as I can, but for now, let's go eat." He playfully patted her butt.

Her stomach chose that moment to growl again, and Jackson couldn't help but laugh. Wrapping his arm around her he guided her back toward their villa and the specially ordered feast. She had no idea what was in store and Jackson's body tensed with anticipation. She wanted a sexy tropical vacation with a stranger and he was the right man to give it to her.

They were both in for the night of a lifetime.

11

A BEAUTIFUL TABLE WITH white linens, silver, crystal, china and tiny votives had been set in front of the windows of the villa where a gentle breeze cooled Mariska's skin. A romantic dinner fit for a queen, but she had issues with the man across from her.

"Okay, Jackson, really. Did you learn nothing from breakfast?" She stuck her fork into a piece of lobster and dipped it in butter. Savoring the tasty goodness, she closed her eyes.

"If you don't stop moaning like that every time you take a bite, we're never going to make it through the meal." His voice was tight with need, and Mar liked that she was responsible for his lack of control. "What do you mean about breakfast?"

"We stuffed our faces at breakfast, and I fell asleep. I refuse to let that happen again." And if they didn't make love soon she would go insane. Or explode from desire. Either way it would be messy.

His blue eyes raked across her face greedily, down to her chest and then back. "Do you really think I have any intention of letting you sleep?"

"I hope not." Her voice came out a whisper. The promise of his words sent her libido into overdrive, and she no longer trusted herself to speak. She took another bite of lobster, licking the butter from her lip with her tongue.

Jackson gave her a strange look. "It's getting chilly in here." Standing, he closed the doors and pulled the curtains closed.

Mar took another bite of lobster and pushed her plate away. "That's it for me. I can't eat any more," she complained.

"I needed to make sure you had plenty of protein to sustain you the next few hours." Jackson's voice was low and sexy.

"Hours?" Mar couldn't hide her excitement.

"Yes. In fact, that's a beautiful dress, but I think it's time you took it off." The words were said so nonchalantly that she wondered if she heard him right. Mariska's heart stopped for a second, her nipples hardened.

"Is that an order, Jackson?" Her voice was deeper and sexier than she'd ever heard it.

His eyes widened with surprise, but he recovered quickly. "Yes, Mariska, it is." His husky tone sent a shiver of delight through her, and it was all she could do not to hop on his lap and ride him into tomorrow.

Standing wasn't easy since her legs had turned to liquid rubber, but she did what he asked, hands shaking slightly as she undid the knot holding up her dress. It fell into a pool of fabric at her feet. She stepped out of it and reached down to put it on the back of the chair. She stood before him, bare-breasted in a lacy black thong and nothing else.

They may have eaten a fabulous meal, but the look in his eyes was one of pure hunger. As the air touched her breasts they tightened even more. She almost put her hands over them, but stopped herself.

He watched her for a moment, taking in the panties and lingering over her chest.

Mariska gave it back to him, pausing when she saw the large bulge in his shorts. She'd already had an effect on him and that knowledge gave her power.

"What do you want me to do now?" She lifted her arms above her head and stretched her back.

She heard his sharp intake of breath. "Lay down on the bed."

Mariska made a show of bending over and pulling down the lightweight blanket and sheets that covered the bed. She propped the pillows in the center of the headboard and then positioned herself against them.

"Is this okay?" She gave him a Cheshire cat grin.

Jackson's eyes devoured her and she couldn't keep the blush from creeping onto her cheeks. "I don't know how you found me, but I'll thank the gods for the rest of my life," he said. "You are one exquisite creature."

Mariska's body trembled with anticipation. Her panties were now drenched and she wondered how long he'd play this game. The only thing she needed was his ginormous cock inside her, pounding away. Ever since she'd touched him this morning, she'd wanted him sliding in and out of her. "I'm pretty sure you were the one who found me," she said playfully.

"Ah. You're right. Good move on my part."

Sliding off his shirt, he stood over her.

Mariska was afraid she'd scream if he didn't hurry.

After moving the rolling table they'd dined on nearer the bed, Jackson lifted the silver top off one of the dessert dishes and revealed warm fruit compote with whipped cream.

"Lose the thong," he said before he turned around.

Again, she did as he ordered, tossing the black lace on the chair where she'd left her dress. She had no idea what he planned but the last thing she desired right then was food.

Jackson stuck his fingers in the dessert and grabbed a slice of kiwi. Sliding it across her lips, he offered it to her. She sucked it off his fingers, licking the juice as she did. He took his middle finger and dipped it into the cream, and then bent down as he painted her pussy with it.

Mariska shuddered with pleasure, her back arching, and his fingers continued their manipulation.

The fire in her lower body built quickly and she moved her hips in motion with his fingers. When he stopped to grab more food, she whimpered.

"No," she cried, her body aching with need.

"No, what?" His fingers stopped a few inches above her heat.

"Jackson, don't stop, please," she begged.

"I have no plans to stop for a very long time." He put whipped cream on her pussy and then devoured her with his mouth. As he sucked and licked her hotness, Mariska shuddered with pleasure over and over. Then his teeth found that tiny nub and worked her so that she bucked against his face. He held her hips in his hands and used his mouth to drive her over the edge.

Mariska could no longer think. All she could do

was feel. When he pumped two fingers into her as he nibbled her, the tension in her body snapped and she rode the wave of pleasure into a shuddering release.

"Ohh." She could say nothing else.

When she finally opened her eyes she saw his hand in the whipped cream again. This time she came the second his teeth found her nub. "Jackson, please. I need you," she growled. She came so hard she grabbed his head and forcibly pulled him up her body.

Jackson moved up over her and kissed her. She could taste the cream mixed with her on his mouth. She reached down to slide her hand around his cock but he pulled away from her. "Not yet, baby."

"Jackson," she begged again. "I need you in me now."

"I know what you need." Grabbing the hot fudge, he dipped a finger in and then teased her mouth. This time she sucked it like she would his cock.

When he groaned, she knew he understood exactly what she wanted.

Finally he removed his finger and dipped it into the hot fudge again, sliding it in circles around her nipples. Then he set the bowl down and lay next to her. His tongue swirled around the nipple, licking her, and when he nipped lightly, her hands fisted the pillows around her.

"Mmm," was all she could say.

His hand slid down and he rubbed his finger on the already overstimulated nub. Between his tongue and his hand she was shuddering with another orgasm in seconds.

"Jackson," she cried out. "Please, now."

Reaching for a condom from the box, he handed it to her. In her excitement she almost couldn't get the package opened. Finally she ripped it open with her teeth.

Before sliding it on, she pushed down the bed so she could taste him. Suckling his cock in the same way he did her tit, sliding her tongue down the length of him. She loved watching him grow even larger and took as much of him as she could into her mouth.

This time it was his hands that went into her hair.

"Mar," he whispered and she knew he fought for control. She wanted him to come in her mouth right then, but she didn't think the rest of her body would forgive her.

Backing off, she pulled the sheath over his now slick cock.

Jackson rose up on his knees and positioned himself between her legs. Lifting them so she could wrap herself around him as he plunged into her. Mariska grabbed the top of the teak headboard with her hands and thrusted against him. They fit so perfectly, it was as if they'd been made for each other.

"Yes," she cried as he pounded in and out, seeming to know that she needed it hard. When he slowed she whimpered again.

"Touch yourself, baby," Jackson ordered.

"No. Jackson, please."

"I will, Mar. But you have to touch yourself for me."

The way those gorgeous bedroom blues begged her there was no way she could ever tell him no. And in that moment she would do anything for him.

Mariska obeyed, letting go of the headboard and running her right hand across her breast and down to her sex, where he began pumping her hard and fast.

The heat in his eyes made her brave and she began rubbing her nub in concert with his thrusts in and out. He pounded her so hard, it was as if every nerve in her body could feel his cock moving inside her, driving her mad. She tightened her legs around him. When he increased the pace and she could feel every inch of him inside her, her body became one tight nerve.

"Come for me, baby. Come on." His words urged her to go faster and faster, her body ached for release. Mariska was so overcome by the sensation that when the orgasm hit she shouted at the top of her lungs.

"Stay with me." His voice strained, he continued to ride her, building her up one more time to a final crescendo that almost made her lose consciousness. She seriously saw stars for a second.

The only thing that centered her was the look of pleasure mixed with possession in Jackson's eyes as he claimed her. Tears burned in her eyes at the joy she saw as he thrust one last time.

She hadn't noticed they spilled over until Jackson suddenly stopped and gave her a guarded stare.

"Did I hurt you? Are you okay?"

At first she couldn't speak and closed her eyes. Her body limp and languid, she remembered to smile.

"I—I am happier than I've ever been in my life." She whispered the words and then reached up to him, pulling him into a kiss.

His furrowed eyebrows said he didn't believe her. "Are you sure?"

"Silly man. I think people in Kentucky know how good I am right now. I only hope no one comes to investigate what we were doing. Did I really scream as loud as I think I did?"

His smile actually reached his eyes. "Yes, you did." She could tell he finally understood that she was beyond okay.

She breathed a happy sigh. "You are wonderful."

"I think the title of wonderful goes to you." He used his thumbs to wipe away the last of the moisture from her cheeks. "Come on, let's go rinse off."

Mar wasn't sure she could get any of her muscles to cooperate. Her body was one giant pleasure puddle. When she didn't move immediately he scooped her up. Thinking he would take them to the shower, she was surprised when he headed to the front door.

"Jackson, what are you doing?"

"I'm going to rinse you off?"

She grabbed his chin with her fingers. "But I'm naked, we both are."

"Do you care, baby? Really? It's dark, and this part of the beach is ours. Let's make the most of it. Besides, we need to clean up fast."

"Why is that?" She gave up her modesty and let him carry her outside.

"We have five more desserts to go." He waggled his eyebrows and ran into the ocean.

Mariska squealed, but it wasn't from the cool water.

12

JACKSON ENVIED MARISKA'S ability to sleep so heavily, as he never caught more than three hours at a time. It was eleven in the morning and she hadn't moved. He couldn't blame her. They'd made love until almost six, and managed to make it through all the desserts. He had to admit that he'd never had a buffet quite like Mariska. Every inch of her was delectable, even without the added sweets.

Studying her delicate face, he remembered the way she looked at him when they made love. Something shattered inside him last night and he was worried it might be the carefully built wall he'd constructed around his heart. How could he have grown to care so much for her in such a short time? He'd intended this to be a fun romantic fling, something easy to walk away from and never look back.

Now he knew that wouldn't happen. Their night had meant more to him than he could have ever imagined, and it went far beyond the incredible sex. There was a deeper connection between them, and he knew she felt it, too. He saw it in her eyes. His heart would pay for it later.

You're no good for her, man. The longer you stay here the worse it's going to be. Get your mind out of this fantasy world and back to reality.

As much as he tried to push that inner voice aside, and wake Mar so they could make love again, he couldn't do it.

He'd been a soldier for too long.

Forcing his thoughts away from the woman beside him, he deliberated about his next move. The thing he needed more than anything was information.

He'd borrow her laptop to check his e-mail. If Dawson had sent him an answer he'd most likely have to leave in a few hours. If he hadn't, he might be able to spare one more day with Mariska. But that was it. Jackson couldn't risk the people who were after him catching up with him here.

It was too dangerous for Mariska. He wasn't sure when it had happened, but her safety was more important to him than his own.

Sliding carefully out of bed, he showered and dressed. Grabbing her computer, he snuck out the door, careful to keep the light from waking her.

After all that sugar, his body craved some protein, and he picked up an egg sandwich and coffee from the hotel breakfast bar. Then he found a small table in the corner that gave him a good view of the room, and sat down to check his account.

"Mr. Greely?" There was a familiar voice to his right. Oh, hell. Jackson didn't look up, but he knew it was Carl Scoggins. The man was the bookkeeper who dealt with several of Vlad's associates. *What the hell is he doing here?* Jackson ignored the man. He had to in order to keep his cover.

"Mr. Greely." Scoggins touched Jackson's shoulder and he had to look up. "It's me, Carl," the slightly balding and very short man said. He was dressed in a pair of wild Bermuda shorts, a white T-shirt, black socks and odd-looking sandals.

Jackson stared at the man blankly. "I'm sorry, you must have me confused with someone else." Jackson gave a brief smile. He used his American accent since Scoggins knew him as a Scotsman, who wanted in on an arms deal. The only upside of this crappy chance meeting was that Jackson had saved the man's life.

Scoggins stared at him for a full thirty seconds. "You look just like Jason Greely, a gentleman I—worked with in London." The other man gave Jackson the once-over again. "You could be his twin. It's the oddest thing."

"Not really." Jackson looked past the man to see if anyone else was with him. "I have one of those faces. My girlfriend thinks I look like one of those film stars. So are you here on vacation?" Jackson did his best to keep his tone light and airy as if was meeting the man for the first time.

Scoggins pursed his lips, and then smiled. "Yes, I came out for a holiday. I had business in Bangkok and decided to come to the coast for a bit of sun. London is a dreary place this time of year."

"Never been there," Jackson lied. If this man had been in Bangkok it meant he'd been in touch with Vlad. Scoggins was the moneyman between Vlad and several arms dealers. He was the one who transferred the funds to accounts after buys. "But I hope to go someday. Well, I'm sorry I'm not your friend. It was nice to meet you." Jackson nodded a farewell and then looked down at his breakfast.

"Yes, nice to meet you, too. Uh. I can't get over the resemblance, though now that I look at you, there are some subtle differences. Your hair color and the scars on your face." Jackson could thank Vlad's men for those marks. "Well, my breakfast is getting cold. I'll see you around." The man walked off and Jackson took a deep breath.

One phone call or text and Jackson would be dead in a matter of hours. Hell. He'd have to find some answers fast and get out of Phuket before Vlad could find him.

His appetite gone, Jackson opened Mariska's computer and signed on. There were two e-mails on the special account, the first from Dawson.

She? No deal. London Friday. Have a solution to difficulty.

Jackson was confused. What the hell did *She? No deal* mean? He tried to think back to the e-mail he sent in the city. He'd thanked the other man for the asset and asked for news.

Oh, hell.

The asset wasn't a woman.

Rubbing the bridge of his nose with his thumb and forefinger, Jackson wondered how he could have screwed up in such a major way. Mariska wasn't the one he was supposed to meet in the bar yesterday. He blew out a breath. He'd thought for sure when he heard the name Stonegate she was it. Now he'd put a poor innocent woman's life in danger for no good reason.

Ass.

Was he that desperate that he'd reach out to the first person who showed him kindness? And she had. She'd been so willing to believe all the lies. The money and her resources had also made him think—what?

God, he really was an idiot. He'd followed her here half hoping he'd figure out what she was supposed to do for him. He grunted. He'd used the poor woman in so many ways it wasn't funny. He felt like crap.

Sipping his coffee, Jackson forced himself to think about this immediate problem. He pushed past his idiotic mistake and concentrated on Dawson's message. He needed to get to London in less than a week.

Finding a way out of Thailand wouldn't be easy. He'd been trying for more than a month. It didn't help that he was on Interpol's list of most wanted. But time was of the essence now. Dawson had a solution, and Jackson would do whatever it took to get his life back.

After opening the second e-mail sent to the account, he found it, too, was in code. A minute later he figured out it was from his friend Pete.

Dawson compromised. Do not trust. Intel has him pegged as source of your troubles. He's the one who called you a traitor. Not a friendly.

Jackson's stomach churned.
What the hell?

Was it possible Dawson had been the one to screw him over?

Pete had been with the Company for more than twenty years and mentored Jackson in the early days. Jackson didn't trust many people, but Pete was one of them. He'd sent Pete a message weeks ago, but when the man didn't reply Jackson figured he didn't intend to get his hands dirty. He couldn't blame the man.

There was a multitude of reasons for an agent to get burned, but Jackson hadn't done any of them as far as he knew. For the past month he'd racked his brain going over each and every day of the last two years while he'd been undercover infiltrating Vlad's gang.

Every time he tried to think of something he could have done that would have been misconstrued, he failed. He'd followed the book—well, as much of a book as there was when you were flying by the seat of your pants and doing your best not to get killed.

Still, there were procedures and he'd followed them. Only checking in with his handler every few months with updates. It had taken almost eighteen months for him to reach Vlad's inner circle and that's when he discovered the human trafficking ring.

A week after he told Dawson what was going on and asked for backup, everything had gone to hell. Not long after that he'd learned he'd been disavowed and accused of treason.

Pete's message explained a great deal. If Dawson were up to no good, he'd probably convinced the Company that Jackson had been the one to compromise the situation. Whatever the hell the situation was, he was no closer to any answers. And if Dawson was involved that was why.

Clever bastard.

Jackson was still alive, which meant someone was on his side, maybe Pete. Usually a burned agent was dead within twenty-four hours. Jackson had lasted two months so far.

Jackson sent Pete another message.

Tell them I want to come in.

Jackson knew Pete might not be able to do that without compromising himself, but he had already gone out on a limb sending him the message about Dawson. Maybe he'd be willing to do this.

If only he could get to headquarters at Langley, he'd turn himself in. He had no problem talking to the bosses. It might land him in a federal pen if they didn't believe him, but Jackson would chance anything for the opportunity to discover the truth. Of course, he had no evidence. Only his side of the story, and Dawson had made certain the Company thought him a bad seed.

Dammit. Jackson shoved a hand through his hair.

Anxiety. He didn't allow himself to feel it often, but for a few moments he wallowed in it. Then he straightened his shoulders.

Get over it, man. You chose the life. You live it.

After disconnecting from the server, Jackson stopped before closing the laptop. He noticed Mariska had several e-mails marked Urgent. Most of those were from the office, and he didn't need to open them to know what they said. He had a pocketful of messages from the front desk in his back pocket. All of them warning Mariska to call immediately.

He isn't who he says he is had been scrawled on the papers from the desk clerk. Jackson smirked. The SIA was on to him.

Until he figured out a way out of Thailand, Jackson decided he'd stay with Mar. She might not be the asset Dawson sent. The more he thought about it the more likely the jerk had sent a hired gun.

Jackson and Mar must have left the bar before the assassin had arrived. He'd come to the bar a half hour early to check it out, and then he'd been lured in by her beauty.

What if? No, it wasn't possible. Mar was no more an assassin than a two-year-old. Besides, she could have killed him a hundred and one ways the night before. He hated that his mind had even gone there, but trust didn't come easy for him. Life had made him hard and suspicious of everyone he met.

No. *We met by sheer happenstance, in the wrong place at the wrong time.* Or perhaps there was a higher power guarding him after all. There was a good chance that Mar had saved his life by asking for his help that night. His heart felt lighter the more he was around her.

He grunted. Maybe she really was his own personal angel.

It was wrong to use her as a temporary cover, but he'd only do it for one more day. Then he'd head back to the city and see what he could arrange in the way of transportation out of this godforsaken place.

There was also the fact, one he didn't want to

examine too closely, that his mind and body demanded to spend more time with her. Last night had been the first occasion in years that he'd felt anywhere close to another human, no longer an unemotional robot. The way she'd given herself to him, and he'd lost himself in her. He'd become addicted to the sound of her voice as she fell over that edge into bliss.

The thought of their being together caused him to tighten with need.

She is most definitely my drug of choice.

He'd stay the day, and then slip out during the cover of darkness. The idea of leaving didn't sit well with him, and he hated the deceit. Even more now that he knew she was never meant to be a part of this. He'd dragged her unwilling into his web of lies.

Something caught his attention on the computer. A red folder marked *priority.* He shouldn't invade her privacy any more than he had, but the spy in him couldn't help it. Clicking on Open, he read her notes about researching and helping out some of the other investigators with their cases. From the copious documents he could see she was thorough and good at working behind the scenes. She didn't give herself enough credit when it came to her investigative skills.

There was also a proof of a new brochure they were designing about the Stonegate Investigative Agency.

After reading about all the players—from the FBI profiler Dr. Liu—he'd actually read some of her books—to forensic anthropologist Patience McGee, another top one in her field—he understood why Mariska worked so hard to keep the agency open. This was an amazing group of investigators, most of them women, all of them noted experts. He couldn't believe her mother had been able to amass so much talent in one place.

People wanted to work with the best, and Mariska's mother was definitely that. God, and he'd put Mar's life in danger with his idiocy.

Something stirred his senses and he smelled Mariska before he saw her come around the corner. That soap she used brought to mind sweet flowers in sunshine.

Shutting down the computer, he smiled at her as she walked in. She'd showered and her wet hair was up in a clip. She wore a sarong over a bikini, this one navy blue. The top had tiny silver studs.

His troubled morning dissipated with one glance at her beautiful face.

"Good morning." Remembering his manners he stood. Leaning down he kissed her lightly on the lips. She tasted of peppermint.

"I missed you." She tugged at his shirt. Then she pushed him back in his seat and pulled out the chair across from him.

As she took in the table, he wondered what she thought when she saw the laptop. Her eyes skipped past the piece of metal and landed on the cup in front of him. "Is that coffee?"

"It is. Would you like me to get you a—"

She picked up his cup and sipped before he could finish. Sighing with pleasure, Mar closed her eyes as if she were drinking manna from heaven.

Opening her eyes again, she picked up his sandwich. "You're done with this, right?"

Before he could answer, she took a bite and he laughed out loud. "Hungry this morning?"

Her mouth full of egg and bread, she shrugged.

"Breakfast is almost over but we could order some lunch." He turned to find a waiter.

Swallowing, she took another sip of his coffee. "Let's get it to go. I want to do something fun today. That is if you're done with your work." She waved a hand over her computer.

"Yes, I'm done. Just checking my e-mails. Did you need it?"

She gave him a delicious smile. "No work for me, buddy. Like I said, I'm here to have fun." She gave him a saucy wink.

"So last night wasn't fun?" He couldn't help kidding with her, and he was more than a little grateful she hadn't seen what he was doing seconds before she walked in.

A blush crept across her cheeks. He loved that about her. That she could seem so innocent, after the wanton creature he experienced last night, made him shift in his seat again.

She reached across and stroked his hand. "Last night was the most incredible experience of any kind I've ever had. It will be etched in the happy part of my brain for the rest of my life."

Jackson squeezed her hand. "I'm messing with you."

She gave him a sweet smile. "Yes, but I want you to know how special it was. And when I make my list of top ten fun things to do, you will be number one."

Jackson pulled her around the table and into his lap.

"It's etched into the happy part of my brain, too." He planted a big kiss on her lips. "Now tell me what this fun thing is you plan to do."

She wiggled against his erection. "After we take care of this," she said, boldly slipping her hand down to his crotch. To anyone walking by they would think she was bracing herself on his legs, but her fingers kneaded his cock, making it difficult to sit still. "Let's go surfing."

That was not what he'd expected to hear. Maybe shopping or looking for shells, but surfing?

"I thought you were kidding yesterday." He finally had to grab her hand and trap it behind her before he embarrassed them both by moaning with pleasure. She had no idea the power she had over him.

Or maybe she did, from that twinkle in her eye. Innocence be damned, she was a tigress and he was her prey.

She shrugged and drew her lips into a pout as if she were upset he'd stopped her fingers.

"Nope. I love surfing. And I checked with the desk. The sharks don't migrate in this area this time of year. So no fear of fins."

He picked her up and sat her back in her chair.

"You're a wicked woman. Now tell me more about the surfing."

She gave him a saucy grin. "I am not wicked, only hungry for more than food." Taking another sip of coffee, she glanced at him over the cup. "To answer your question I learned how to surf a couple of years ago. I'm not great, but I can hold my own. The waves are stellar out there today and I'm in the mood to get crazy."

Jackson was a fairly good surfer, though he hadn't done it in a while. Not since he had an assignment in Australia almost three years ago.

"I asked at the front desk, and we can rent boards from the hotel. So you up for it?"

He gave her a wicked grin. "Oh, I'm up for it."

She slapped at his hand. "You are a bad, bad man. And I think it's time for you to be punished." She stood up. "I'm going to go rent the boards. You order me some lunch and meet me in the room."

Grabbing her wrist, he stopped her.

"First, there's something you need to tell me."

"What is it?" She frowned, seemingly surprised by his sudden change in tone.

"How many people are in the restaurant?"

The question caught her off guard, but he watched as the realization of what he was really asking spread over her face.

Staring straight into his eyes, she told him, "Besides you and me, there are five guests. Most of them chatting, as they finished breakfast a long time ago. There are two waiters and a busboy standing off to the side, ready for everyone to clear up. Probably because they have to get the lunch buffet set up, but I'm sure their orders are to keep everything out until we leave."

A twinkle lit her eyes. "Satisfied?"

"Proud. You're a fast learner."

Giving him a tweak of the ear, she leaned down and kissed him. "Don't be late, or your punishment is going to be very, very bad." She leaned on him so that her hand could slide down his cock, and her breasts were shoved in his face. A moment later she sashayed away.

Jackson flagged down a waiter, grateful there was a tablecloth to hide the hard evidence her hand had caused. She would pay for that. Oh, yes, he'd make her pay over and over again.

13

JACKSON SAT ON HIS surfboard in the warm ocean water watching Mariska. She was certainly more comfortable on the board than he was. He'd grown rusty, and for some reason, possibly because they'd had mind-blowing sex twice in a row less than an hour ago, he had a tough time staying on the board after riding a couple of waves.

Mariska was more than competent when it came to the sport, and following her slicing through the waves was one big turn-on. The woman rode a curl like no one's business, and she was so damn sexy in that blue bikini he wanted to ravage her right there in the middle of the wave.

Catching her attention before she paddled out again, he waved that he was going in, hoping that she would follow suit. He really needed to kiss her.

She held up a finger, indicating she wanted to ride once more.

Jackson felt denied, but pulled his board onto the beach. Stepping into the white tent he'd arranged, he glanced around at the round bed, and the pillows strewn on the floor. They were on one of the private beaches, and he'd paid extra to make sure it stayed that way. Mariska had smiled and expressed how impressed she was with him in arranging such a fabulous treat so quickly.

He grabbed a Coke from the basket of food and drinks the hotel had provided. Trying to replenish his energy. He didn't want to risk missing her surf, so he stepped back outside with his drink.

Mariska paddled out and let a couple of waves pass. Then of course she picked the biggest one they'd seen all day. Jackson watched with a mixture of fear and awe as she rode through the curl. It was nothing short of perfection.

Every time he thought he had a handle on her, she would say or do something that threw him off track. Thoughtful and sweet, there was also a bit of an edge to her. They'd both been alone a great deal as children and Jackson wondered if perhaps that was why he felt so connected to her.

He watched as she crested a wave and stood on her board. The way she rode it was one of the sexiest things he'd ever witnessed. Her feet slid up the board as she adjusted her balance and her arms lifted horizontally.

Jackson's body heated as he remembered those arms and legs wrapped around him. The way her body moved against his, and that mouth of hers. He'd never tire of the way she kissed him.

She rode the board until it slid into the sand with a gentle splash.

"You lied." He winked as she unhooked the ankle strap keeping the board tied to her.

"I don't lie." She grabbed the soda from his hand and took a long swig. "Okay, maybe sometimes, but only when the job calls for it. You have to clue me in to what I did this time."

Grabbing her around the waist, he pulled her toward him. "You're an amazing surfer. You didn't fall once. I'm kind of jealous."

She slapped playfully at his chest. "That's because I didn't try to be all macho and take the biggest wave of the day, and hello! You hung in there till the end of the curl. That's something."

He kissed her forehead. "How do you do that?"

She shrugged. "What?"

"I've never met anyone who works so hard to make the people around her feel better about themselves."

She gave him a very unladylike snort. "That's because you don't hang out with the right people."

Damn, she'd hit that one right. Everyone he knew was out for themselves. There wasn't a single person he could trust, and there was certainly no one who would lift him up the way she did. This time with her was more precious than even he had realized, and he intended to make the most of it.

"Hey—" She touched his cheek. "Whatever you're thinking. Stop it. This afternoon is for frolic." She batted her eyelashes at him and he couldn't help but laugh.

"So, how does one commence this frolicking?" He twisted a strand of her wet hair gently around his finger. "Would it start like this?" He leaned down and kissed her neck. "Or maybe like this?" Cupping her right breast, he thumbed her nipple to attention.

"Mmm." She groaned and shoved her pelvis into his erection, grinding her hips against him. "Yes. I'd say you catch on quick." She pushed him toward the opening of the tent. "I think it's time to make use of this sheikh and princess setup you have going here."

"Sheikh?" He nipped at her neck again, and then let her push him toward the mouth of the tent.

"Yes. You are the handsome and mysterious sheikh. You've plied me with wine—" she held up the can of soda "—and now you're going to have your way with me." She shoved him down on the bed, set the Coke on a nearby table and then crawled on top of him.

"I'm going to have my way with you?" His voice was hoarse as she moved her pussy against his erection. The warmth of her nearly made him come right then, but he forced himself to breathe and relax.

"Or vice versa. Does it really matter?" She gave him a wicked grin as she tugged off her bikini top, her pert breasts bouncing as she bent down to untie the string on his board shorts.

"No, it doesn't matter at all," he said as he leaned up so he could take one of those breasts into his mouth, suckling the nipple until it was a hard peak.

She gasped and pushed herself farther into his mouth. As he suckled the other breast, he slid a finger into her bikini bottoms and into her pussy, pumping in and out, until he felt her shudder with release. Lifting her off of him, he put her gently onto the bed and pulled the bottoms off.

Expecting to see pleasure when he looked up, he was surprised by the worried look in her eyes. "What is it?" He was instantly beside her, drawing her to him.

"Are you sure, um, that it's private?" she whispered. "I'm not so sure I can be quiet. I tend to lose any sense at all when you're around."

He chuckled and kissed her hard on the lips. "It's private, baby. I promise. You are free to do whatever you want." Moving down her naked body, he tongued her nub until she writhed and was shoving her wetness into his face. She was sweet as always, mixed with the salt of the sea. Nothing short of intoxicating, better than a full-bodied wine on a warm night.

"Oh, God, Jackson, please." Her hands fisted the sheets and he slid two fingers in her pussy as he continued to nibble and lick. She bucked against him and her body shuddered again.

Jackson could wait no longer. He slid off his shorts and reached for one of the condoms he'd put under a pillow. Then he reached for her and slid her to the edge of the bed; wrapping her legs around his shoulders he lifted her hips and plunged into her. She met his pace, thrusting herself against him.

It was fast and furious and he didn't care. From the moans he gathered she didn't, either. Everything he felt for her went into those thrusts. She watched him with such intensity, and he her, as if they both knew this was something else. Something special. His cock exploded inside her as she screamed her own release. Jackson had promised her privacy, but there was a good chance people on the other side of the island had heard her.

He couldn't help but chuckle.

"What's so funny?" She scooted back on the pillows as he disposed of the condom.

Jackson moved beside her, kissing her neck. He

wouldn't dare call attention to her scream. He was certain she wasn't aware that she even did it. It gave him such pleasure to know he could drive her to such extremes. "I tend to lose myself when I'm around you. That went a little faster than I'd planned."

Snuggling against him, her chin under his chest felt so perfect. "That was a two-way street, buddy," she playfully chided. "I wanted it hard and fast, and that's what you gave me."

"I aim to please, ma'am." He gave her his best Southern drawl.

She snorted again. He loved it when she did that.

"Well, I'd say that aim of yours is dead-on. I don't think I've ever—" She stopped herself.

"What is it?" He pulled away so he could see her face.

Rolling her eyes, she tried to duck her head again, but he held on to her chin.

"You can tell me, Mar. Anything. I'm the last person to judge."

She smiled at him. "I get that from you. You have a way of sizing up people and situations, but you're probably the least judgmental man I've ever met. Even with Gladstone. You gave him some tough love, but you didn't make him feel small, which is what most people would do."

Jackson sighed. "You're changing the subject. This isn't about me. It's about you. What were you going to say?"

"Darn, and I thought I was doing so good with the deflecting."

He pushed her still-damp hair behind her ears. "Say it, Mar. Whatever it is."

"I've never had orgasms like this." She said it as a whisper. "I mean, I've had decent sex, I guess. But never the mind-blowing stuff people talk about. Until now."

Part of him was proud that he'd been able to bring her such joy. But the other part was angry when he thought of her with another man. *Hold it. You're no saint.* She'd told him that no other man had made her feel the way he did. He'd focus on that for now. But he understood what she'd meant. There was something between them that he'd never experienced before, either.

"See, now I'm totally embarrassed. I can see it on your face, you think I'm ridiculous." She started to sit up, and he grabbed her arm.

"You are many things. Beautiful," he said as he kissed her lips. "Smart," he said as he kissed her forehead. "And sexy as hell," he said as he nibbled her earlobe. "But never ridiculous."

She shook her head. "You're saying that to make me feel better."

"No. If it makes you feel any better, it's not always been like this for me, either."

That made her frown.

"What's wrong now?"

She screwed up her face. "See, it kills me to think you've been with another woman. That's what I'm talking about. I've only known you a couple of days. I swear to you I'm not some stalker chick. There's a connection with you. I don't know why. Maybe because you seem to know exactly how to push the right buttons with me."

"I wouldn't mind it." Jackson waggled an eyebrow at her.

She frowned again. "What the hell are you talking about now?"

"You, as a stalker. That might be kind of fun. You could follow me around in that bikini you were wearing earlier and hide behind bushes. Maybe show up on my doorstop naked. I'm seeing some real possibilities here."

She snorted again, and he couldn't help but laugh out loud.

"You really should do that more often." She touched his cheek again, this time her eyes tender with something he didn't quite understand. "Your laugh makes me warm from my head to my toes."

Jackson had done more laughing with her in the last few days than he had in years. "Hmm. Are you warmer here?" He slid his hand across her flat belly. Then lower. "Or here?"

She pulled him into a kiss. "You ask too many questions, Jackson."

It had been almost ten minutes since her last mind-blowing orgasm. Jackson decided it was time to make her scream with pleasure again.

THEIR AFTERNOON OF LOVEMAKING had worn them both out. Jackson had managed a few hours of sleep. Mar was sleepy when they'd returned to the villa, and she had asked for a couple of hours to rest some more, and to freshen up before their dinner date.

Jackson had spent the last half hour arranging for them to eat on the rooftop of the hotel, in a private area where they would be close to the moon and stars. He was stepping out onto the path when he saw Scoggins heading his way. It was too late for him to turn around without being rude, so he smiled. "Good evening," he said as the man stopped in front of him. Jackson wanted to push past, but he paused.

Jackson could feel the tension rolling off the other man, whose earlier smile had turned into a grim expression. Something was up.

Expecting the worst, Jackson readied for action by shifting his weight to his back foot, and reaching for the knife he'd tucked into his waist.

Scoggins held up two hands in a stop motion. "Stand down, man. I mean you know harm. I thought you might like to know about an interesting telephone conversation I had with one of my associates."

Jackson shrugged nonchalantly but kept his hand on the hilt of the knife. "Really? Someone I might know?" He knew the charade was up, but Jackson wasn't quite ready to give in.

Scoggins gave him a hard look. "Oh, I'd say we know a few of the same people. One of them in particular seems quite set on finding a man fitting your description."

Damn. It was done. He had to get the hell out of here. Hell, he had to get Mar to a plane, and then lose himself somewhere else in Thailand. Find a way to Langley.

"I suppose you mentioned that you'd seen me?" Jackson could kill the man, he was that pissed off, but Scoggins's death would serve no purpose.

Scoggins shook his head. "No, actually, I didn't. Whoever you are, and whatever you are mixed up in with those devils in Bangkok is no concern of mine. They still owe me millions, and don't seem in a hurry to pay. And I seem to remember that man matching your description, the twin I was telling you about? Well, he saved my life back in London, and arranged it so that I could continue to do business without worrying about the authorities. I promised that man loyalty, and I never go back on my word."

Jackson breathed for the first time in what seemed like several minutes. "How can I trust you?"

"As I recall, you don't trust anyone. Can't say I blame you. But I mean what I say. It serves me no purpose to turn you in, you can look at it that way if it makes you feel better. But the truth is, I never welsh on my debts. And I owe you my life. I'd be in prison for life, or dead, if it weren't for you. We'll leave it at that." Scoggins moved past, but Jackson caught his arm.

"How long?"

Scoggins cocked his head to the side. "They think you're still in the city. You have a couple of days at least. But you need to get out of this country. Vlad has people everywhere and it won't be long before they find you." He waved a hand toward the ocean. "Even here."

"Thanks."

"You would have done the same for me. And besides, I'm still working in London. Perhaps we'll do business again some day."

Jackson nodded. Scoggins walked into the hotel, leaving him on the sidewalk. Staring out into the ocean a myriad of thoughts ran through his head. Where should he go next? Could he get Mar to a major airport? They might be watching, and her safety was the priority. He needed to get a look at that laptop again.

Guilt assailed him. He couldn't stand that he was being so deceitful with her, but there was no way around it. That laptop was the only way he could communicate with the outside world.

In his mind he promised himself that he would do whatever it took to protect her. Unfortunately, that didn't make him feel any less guilty.

14

SOMETHING TUGGED MARISKA from a deep sleep. Pulling her toward consciousness when all she wanted was to stay in her dreams with Jackson.

"Wake up. Come on, sleepyhead. Open those eyes." Jackson's sexy voice coaxed her back to reality. "Please, baby. I have a surprise for you."

Slipping farther down in the warmth of the bed seemed a much better idea. She'd spent a little too much time surfing and in the sun, and now she was paying for it. It didn't help that she and Jackson had made love for hours. Her mind and body were exhausted. A dull ache had formed in her head, and her skin felt tight, even though she'd showered and applied lotions before crawling between the cool sheets. But he sounded excited and she couldn't stand disappointing him.

She opened a sliver of an eye. "Happy now?" she said grumpily as she pulled the sheet back over her face. The dim light in the room was enough to make her blink.

Jackson wore a dress shirt, dark slacks and one of his devastating smiles. "You look gorgeous," he said as he moved in for a kiss.

She held a hand over her mouth. "Stop. I have sandpaper mouth. You can't kiss me right now."

"Hmm." He tugged her hand away. "I'll decide if I can kiss you or not. And can't say I've ever heard of sandpaper mouth. Is that some tropical disease I should be worried about?"

"I refuse to kiss you until I've brushed my teeth. And if a cat has ever licked you, then you know exactly what sandpaper mouth is." She pushed the sheet off her and stood naked before him. A few days ago she would have been self-conscious about her body, but now she was only worried about her breath.

Jackson refused to let her pass, and planted a big kiss on her lips. "I say you taste perfect, sandy mouth and all." His hands slipped down her bottom and pulled her to him. "And you feel perfect." His hands slipped around her hips and settled there.

"I thought you said you had a surprise for me?" She wiggled away from him, determined to brush the grime from her tongue before he could kiss her again.

He looked confused for a moment, then he smiled. "Seeing you naked sent the past hour straight out of my head. I do have a big surprise for you."

She turned her head and smiled up at him. "Um, I think I've seen that surprise already. Over, and over, and over again. Not that I'm complaining." She boldly cupped him and could feel his cock growing in her hand.

"Talk about a one-track mind." He gently removed her hand and pushed her toward the bathroom. "You need to get ready. Your surprise is waiting at the hotel."

She clapped her hands together. "Normally, I'm not a big fan of surprises, but now I can't wait. I'll be fast." She turned back at the door and caught him frowning at the floor, his chin in his hand. "Jackson?"

He glanced up and smiled at her. But she knew she'd seen genuine worry on his face. "Yes? No more stalling. Do your womanly things, hurry, hurry." He shooed her into the bathroom before she could ask what was wrong.

"I only wanted to know what to wear."

"Doesn't matter," he said, "you look beautiful in everything."

That made her laugh as she stared in the mirror. It was crazy that her hair could be a frizzy mess on top of her head and overly pink cheeks, and he thought she was beautiful. She wouldn't dwell on that look on his face. The one that made her worry that perhaps this fantasy was going to end sometime soon.

She turned on the faucets. Her stomach tightened at the thought of him leaving.

"No," she whispered. "The deal is, I enjoy whatever time I have with him. I knew that going in. No regrets."

JACKSON'S SURPRISE HAD BEEN incredible. As they stood on the rooftop of the hotel looking out on to the ocean she felt like she could touch the moon and the stars.

"I don't think I would ever tire of this view," she said softly as she snuggled against his chest. They'd had a el-egant candlelit dinner by the rooftop pool, and Jackson had even arranged for music to stream in through the speakers. She'd learned it came from his iPod, which was connected to the sound system. It was an array of everything from big band to indie rock, and all points in between. It was as eclectic and diverse as the man holding her.

He sighed against her. They had two bottles of wine, and an assortment of local delicacies. She'd eaten more than she'd intended, but she felt more relaxed than she had in years. Jackson had been so attentive, as if he wanted her to remember this night forever.

She would.

But there was a small part of her that couldn't let go of that moment back at the villa. She'd seen the look on his face. He was worried about something, but he wanted her to have this night. She couldn't take that away from him.

"Mmm. This has been just about the most perfect date a woman could ever imagine." She took a deep breath. "Jackson, you can surprise me anytime you want. In fact I may have to change the way I look at surprises from here on out."

When she glanced up at him there was a strange expression on his face. Why couldn't the man take a compliment? "Seriously, I'll be spoiled from now on. No man is ever going to live up to the measure of the Jackson standard." She gave him a grin, but his brows drew together and he wore a deep frown.

"What's wrong?"

"Nothing." He looked angry for some reason. "I need some coffee. I'm going to find the waiters and see if they can bring some up. I'll only be gone a few minutes. I promise."

Before she could answer, he was through the door

leading to the hotel elevator. Something she said had been misconstrued. She thought about her comments and realized he thought she was talking as if they had some kind of future.

Dammit. Jackson. I didn't mean it the way you think.

The wary look in his eyes hadn't been anger—he wanted to escape. How many times had he said he had to move on and that he'd be traveling soon? This was supposed to be a fun weekend with no ties.

The hurt strangled her lungs, until she didn't think she could breathe. Suddenly she felt very alone.

Hell, there's a good chance he's on his way to Bangkok and out of your life right now.

"If he comes back, I won't mention a word about the future. Please, give me one more night with the man," she said to the heavens. "Please, let him come back. I'm not ready to say goodbye. I need more time."

She sniffled. "Jackson, I need you."

Maybe she was tired. Maybe it was too much sun, but she couldn't stop the tears from spilling over.

JACKSON STARED AT HIMSELF in the copper-colored elevator doors.

Coward.

The second she mentioned anything about the future he'd bolted like a bull with an open gate. It wasn't that he hadn't been thinking the same thing. A future with Mar invaded his thoughts more often than not the last few hours. He'd come to realize that she had become the most important person in his life.

That was the rub.

He couldn't allow himself to think that way. It wasn't a good idea for either of them. Then she made the comment about him taking care of her any time, and he'd panicked. He wanted to be there *always* to take care of her, to hold on to her and never let go.

When she mentioned future men who would be compared to him, he'd almost come unglued. He wanted to grab her right then and tell her that no other man would ever touch her. That he was the only man for her.

The feeling was so strong it freaked him out. He'd never felt so possessive about anyone, hell, anything. The idea that she would share those passionate kisses and her gorgeous body with some other man sent his mind and body into turmoil.

Jackson was determined to be the only man she would ever need.

That's not going to happen.

For one millisecond he considered telling her the truth. Explaining why he couldn't be around much longer—assassins could be around any corner. He'd be lucky if he lived through the next weekend.

He knew he wouldn't.

Stop being a desperate loser. The last thing she needs to know is your secrets. Then you really will get her killed.

Jackson found the maître d' at the restaurant, who had arranged the special dinner upstairs. "Would it be possible to have coffee sent up?"

"Yes, sir." The man took the money Jackson offered.

"If you don't mind. Give us about twenty minutes." Jackson would need to come up with some plausible explanation for why he acted like such an idiot. Mar hadn't meant anything by talking about the future. She only wanted to show her appreciation.

The maître d' nodded. "Of course. Would you also like a dessert tray?"

The idea of food turned Jackson's stomach, but he knew how much Mar loved sweets. "Sure. Whatever you think works. But twenty minutes, okay?"

Jackson turned.

"Did she like it?" the man asked.

Jackson gave him a confused look.

"Your wife? Did she enjoy the meal?"

His wife?

Why didn't that scare the hell out of him like it should?

Because you care about her, idiot.

He'd been a jerk to leave her like that.

"She loved it. Thanks." Jackson walked quickly to the elevator, berating himself as it climbed the eight floors to the rooftop.

In his life he'd seen so much violence and corruption, but nothing had ever prepared him for what he viewed when he opened the door and stepped out onto the rooftop. Mar was sitting at the table wiping a tear from her cheek.

"Baby, what's wrong?"

Her sobs intensified and her shoulders shook. Her face was hidden from him and finally he pulled her hands away so that he could see her.

"Tell me." He whispered the words, brushing her hair away from her tear-streaked face.

She hiccupped.

"I'm sorry I left like that. The coffee will be here in a bit. I should have just called down."

Mar put her hand on his heart. "Jackson." The word came out on a shudder. "I don't need coffee. I need you."

The words hit him like a sucker punch to the gut. No one had ever needed him. No one he'd ever cared about had said those words to him. He kissed her head. "I'm here, baby. Tell me what's wrong."

She sat up a little straighter and he handed her a tissue from the side table. "It's silly. I—I thought you left. You ran out of here so fast when I accidentally mentioned the future, and I thought I spooked you. I promise you, I'm not expecting anything past this weekend. But I'm not ready for it to be over yet. I—I didn't want you to leave without saying goodbye."

The last part of the wall around his heart fell away. She cared for him as much as he did her. The practical side of him knew he'd soon have no choice but to leave, but not right now.

"Babe, why would you think that?" He touched her chin with his finger. "I would never leave without saying goodbye to you."

Mar blotted her nose with the tissue. "But when you left—you had this really weird look on your face. You can't fool me. Something I said freaked you out."

Her breath hitched and she coughed a little. "I don't have any desire to leave you, Mar." That part was true. "But—there is something you should know. I—will have to leave soon. You know as well as I do that neither of us is safe as long as we stay in Thailand. I guess when you said something about the future it made me think that we really don't have much more time together."

"You're a really good liar, Jackson. But you forget I do have one talent besides my awesome surfing skills. I can read people."

Jackson dragged his chair next to hers and held her hand. She definitely had acquired that talent. Still, he didn't want to discuss it right then. "Mar, let's enjoy the night. You have your moon and your stars."

She took her hand back and stood to face him. "No. I need to say this to you now because I don't know when you're going to leave," she demanded. "And I'm sorry if it scares you, but I'm not sure I'll ever be ready for you to go." Her voice trembled.

"Mar, honey."

She held up a hand and took a settling breath. "You—you made me care, and that's a good thing in so many ways. I'd reached a point where the only thing that brought me any joy was work. I didn't feel like I fit in with the rest of the world. I know it's crazy, and I expect nothing from you, but I feel like I fit when you're around."

When she put her hand on his cheek he shattered into a million pieces. The confession was the single most intimate moment anyone had ever shared with him. He put his hand over hers and pulled it against his heart.

"I'm going to be more honest than I should. I want to promise you forever after, Mar, more than anything in the world. But I'm not in a place where I can do that. My life is complicated right now, and I honestly never know what the new day will bring."

He stopped, choosing his words carefully. "These

few days with you have been the most amazing in my life. I don't have a clue what my future holds, but I will cherish this time we have. And I care about you. When I do have to leave, it will be with a heavy heart. I promise you." Jackson had no idea where all that had come from, but it surprised him that he meant it all. He'd become so used to lying to get out of situations that he was surprised by how good speaking the truth felt.

"That might be the sweetest thing anyone has ever said to me." She wiped her eyes again. "There's one thing I have to know before we go any further with this. I'd appreciate if you'd be honest. It won't change how I feel about you, but it is something that I have to know."

"I'll tell you if I can." Jackson worried. What if she asked about something concerning his job? He wouldn't lie to her unless he had to. She deserved answers if he could give them to her.

"Are you married?"

Jackson was caught so off guard that he burst out laughing harder than he had in a long time.

Mar gave him a stern look. "I don't think it's that funny."

"You are precious." He left his chair and kissed her cheeks, nose and lips before he answered her. "No, I am not married. I've never been married. And I'm not the kind of guy who would sleep with you if I were." Happy that he could be honest, he pulled her close again.

"Whew. I didn't think so. I mean I may not be that great a detective but I hadn't noticed a ring. Though a lot of guys don't wear them. But I wasn't super excited about being the other woman."

Jackson moved her hair behind her ear. "You are the only woman." Then he kissed her, tasting her as if it were the first time.

Mar's arms curled around his neck, her tongue slipped around his and he knew she wanted him as much as he did her. Then he remembered. Jackson drew back. "Honey, we can't. The coffee is on the way."

Her face scrunched and he could see the wheels turning. She wasn't one to give up easily when she wanted something. He needed a diversion.

Jackson gave her a quick smile. "Dance with me, Mar. Please."

They moved in each other's arms as if they'd been doing it for years. Holding her in that moment would be burned into his brain for eternity. Hell, the last few days really would be ones he would never forget.

He might have been conflicted about what was best for her, but he'd do anything to protect her. Even though he knew that meant leaving her as soon as possible. "No matter what the future holds," he whispered against her hair, "you know I only want what is best for you."

"I know." She gave him the most alluring smile he'd ever seen. "You're my white knight in board shorts." She winked at him, and solidified her place in his heart.

15

THE DAY HAD TAKEN A toll on Mar, and Jackson watched as she slept, waiting until she was deep under before slipping out of the bed. A strange noise in the armoire had him wandering toward it. He discovered the culprit in Mar's purse. Her phone's battery had died. She'd probably forgotten all about it. He found her charger and plugged it in, noticing as he did she had twenty new text messages.

He shouldn't have, but he pushed the buttons so he could read them. Most of the urgent missives were from her friends Chi and another investigator, Katie, at the agency, telling Mar that Jackson Thomas did not exist. Mr. Thomas, the man who was supposed to help her in Bangkok, was an elderly Asian man with six children.

That she had asked them to check him out didn't surprise Jackson. She would have been an idiot not to tell her friends she was going off with a stranger. He was grateful that they cared enough about her to make sure she was safe.

He'd tossed the messages from the front desk in the

trash, but Jackson knew they would continue to worry if she didn't answer. He also didn't have any desire to deal with the truth right then. They'd already tried sending messages through the hotel, next they'd be sending the authorities if they hadn't already.

He couldn't let that happen.

He texted them both back pretending to be Mar.

Having the time of my life. I know all about Jackson, he came clean. Only checking the phone every few days. Don't worry. See you soon.

He wasn't sure it was possible for him to feel guiltier, but he did.

He only had one more day with her. Then he'd leave and she'd never have to know the truth about him. Oh, she would be upset, even more so when she found out that he'd tricked her. But no one would be able to take this time they had away from either of them.

He couldn't risk her finding the messages so he turned the phone off and hid it in his things. Before he left, he'd make sure it was in place where she could find it.

Taking her computer from his bag, he put it down on the table by the windows.

Opening the laptop, he checked for messages from Dawson or Pete. His jaw tightened as he thought about what Dawson had done to him. He wondered if maybe he should go to London. Now that he knew about the other man's deception, he could set a trap of his own and settle this once and for all.

Hell, he'd been accused of treason thanks to the ass.

The anger boiled inside of him, and Jackson had to force himself to calm down. While his hands around Dawson's neck seemed the most logical solution, there were too many variables. Unfortunately, he couldn't know for sure how much Pete really understood about what had happened. There was a slight chance Dawson's actions had been misinterpreted, but Jackson doubted it.

London, hell, Europe in general wasn't a safe place for someone in his predicament. He had a kill order hanging over his head, and operatives from agencies all over the world would take advantage of it.

There wasn't a person in the world he could trust.

Jackson was more determined than ever to find a way back to Langley. It seemed his only option. Funny how a few days could change everything.

Hell, funny how Mar had changed everything. She gave him the will to live. To fight for whatever life he could possibly have. If he could make it to Virginia, that *if* being a big one, he'd at least find out the truth about why they burned him.

Well, Dawson had something to do with it, but he still didn't understand how he'd been set up, or even what the Company knew. Pete might have discovered Dawson was crooked, but that didn't mean anyone else had the information. Pete liked to play things close to the vest, and he wouldn't go to his superiors until he had proof.

Jackson's biggest worry was that someone would kill him before he had the chance to explain to the bosses what had happened, or at least his version of it.

The wind picked up outside, but nothing matched the

fury Jackson felt. His stomach roiled as his mind raced to find an answer. If he desired any kind of future with her, there was only one thing he could do.

After finding the Web site he needed, he did something so desperate he had to push Send before he thought about it too much. He posted an ad, one the Company could decipher.

WRAPPED IN A ROBE FROM the hotel, Mar watched as the sun rose over the horizon. Jackson sat beside her. Both of them held steaming cups of coffee. Everything smelled fresh this morning, as if the ocean tide had wiped away any trace of the day before.

It was a new beginning.

Unfortunately for Mar, it felt like the end. Jackson had been so attentive, waking her so they could see the sunrise. That didn't seem so strange, but when he asked if she had an interest in snorkeling or checking out the village nearby, she knew something was up. Jackson was not the sightseeing type.

"We can do whatever you want," he told her. "The pond where we can snorkel is on the other side of the resort. We can take a small golf cart, and I'm told the fish are amazing. Oh, and I have it on good authority that there are absolutely no sharks." He'd prattled on planning out their adventures and that's how she knew.

It's our last day together.

As she sipped the coffee, she tried not to contemplate what that meant. Oh, he cared about her, but he'd said his life was complicated. If he was in trouble she might be able to help. It wasn't as if she didn't have some incredible resources.

Mar drew her knees up to her chin, and covered them with the robe. Blinking back tears, she was grateful she'd pulled on her sunglasses to hide some of her pain.

She wouldn't dwell on the end. The time she had was precious and she wouldn't waste it on could-haves or would-haves.

"I wouldn't mind snorkeling in the lagoon. But if it's okay with you, I'd kind of like to lay around and work on my tan." She tried desperately to sound nonchalant. She didn't want him to know that she'd realized what was going on. In a weird way, it was her gift to him, an amazing last day together without weepy goodbyes.

He grinned at her and her heart nearly fell out of her chest. "I told you, this is your day. You deserve whatever your gorgeous heart desires."

God, I wish that was the real reason, Jackson. You beautiful liar, you.

Mar chewed on the inside of her lip to keep from crying, and looked back toward the sunrise so he wouldn't see the stupid tears that threatened to slide down her face. She wasn't normally one who shed them easily.

Once the enormous orange orb made its entrance, Mar stood up and kissed the top of his head. "Thank you for that. It's such a peaceful and beautiful way to start the morning. I'm in serious need of a shower. I don't suppose I could talk you into joining me?" Hey, if it were the last day, she would absolutely make the best of it. "I mean, I might need help soaping up my back or something."

He glanced at her, a certain gleam in his eyes, and she knew that he'd taken the bait. Thank Gawd. Her body had been screaming for him since he'd kissed her awake this morning.

"Are you sure?" he asked her carefully.

"I don't know, Jackson. If you can't handle it, I totally understand. Maybe you're tired. We've had a lot of sex. Hmm. I thought you would have recovered by now, but I understand if you don't feel like you can perform." She blew him a kiss. "I'm a big girl, I can shower alone if I have to."

Reaching up, he captured her arm. "Have I mentioned you're a wicked woman?"

She leaned over, sliding her hands down his chest and all the way to his cock. "I think you might have said something about that." She ran her palm down the hard length of him. "But I need a little TLC, the kind only you can provide." After nibbling his ear, she gave the tip of his cock a soft pinch.

Jackson jumped up, and followed her into the villa.

There were ten different spray heads and water splashed from every direction. He helped her out of the robe. When he slipped the T-shirt over her head, her nipples perked to attention. He laved each one with his tongue and then kissed them.

Mar had no desire to wait a minute longer. She untied his board shorts and slid them down his hips.

Jackson picked her up and put her under the sprays. The warm water instantly relaxed her muscles.

"I'll be right back, don't start without me," he said as he left the bathroom. He returned with a foil package.

As soon as he stepped in she grabbed for his cock,

but he moved his hips away from her. "We're doing this my way. Turn around." Taking her soap, he began with her neck. Each time he soaped and then rinsed her, he would land tiny kisses in the area. He worked his way down her neck and back. Then he turned her to face him and began the same process on her front.

He reached her nipples, and suckled each one and then soaped her stomach and pussy. When he bent down and stuck his tongue into her heat and nibbled her clit, Mar wasn't sure she could stand much longer.

The warm water beat against her front and back in rhythm with Jackson's tongue and teeth. Jackson moved her again so that she was braced on the wall. Reaching up, she grabbed the ledge from the window to keep herself steady as he continued to use his teeth. When he slid two fingers into her and began pumping in and out, she bucked against him.

Once again she was lost in a haze of pleasure, every nerve in her body begging for release. "Jackson, please. I need you inside me. Now." She growled out the words.

Jackson stood and kissed her hard. Reaching behind her, he opened the foil package and slid the condom on. "Wrap your legs around me, baby." Helping her, he positioned her so that his cock slid easily into her folds, filling her so completely. He didn't tease her this time. Thrusting in and out, he began pounding her harder and harder.

"Yes." The warm water came from the sides, hitting her nipples in the right spot as he rammed his cock into her. "I want you so bad," she cried. "So bad."

"Not half as bad as I do you." He thrust in hard,

showing her. He kissed her, his tongue following the same movements of his cock, and Mariska rode higher and higher.

"Jackson, ohhh. Yes. I'm—" Words left her as her body shattered into an orgasm so intense she had to let go of the ledge and wrap her arms around his neck to keep from falling.

Jackson came in the same instant and turned so that now his back was against the wall, as if he needed to support them both. If his knees felt anything like the rest of her body, she understood.

"Oh, Mar," he said before he kissed her again.

They stood like that for a few minutes, letting the water run down their bodies.

After turning off the water, he toweled off her body. He tried to give her back her T-shirt, but she tossed it onto the towel rack.

Mar moved toward the bed naked and slipped into the sheets. "Jackson?"

He stood at the doorway watching her.

"What is it?"

Mar smiled at him and reached out. "I really don't want to go snorkeling today."

A grin slid across his face. Drying himself off as he walked toward her, he threw the towel on the chair and climbed in beside her. "Me, either."

16

AMAZING HOW FAST ONE could develop a habit. Jackson loved watching Mar sleep. With her hair splayed out against the pillow he thought again how she looked like a peaceful angel.

Hell, maybe *angel* wasn't the right word for her. *Wicked she-devil* might be more appropriate. They'd spent the entire day in bed, napping and pleasuring one another. They'd made love two more times after the shower, and he still couldn't get enough of her. She'd protested this evening when he insisted she eat something and rest.

When he promised strawberry pie for dessert she finally acquiesced. He'd eaten every last bite off her and then she finally went to sleep.

Slipping his arm from around her waist, he paused when she stirred. The last thing he wanted to do was wake her.

Sliding out of bed, he quickly packed his bag.

You're a damn coward.

The idea of saying goodbye to her face-to-face was too painful. She'd try to be brave and the moment would break both of their hearts. He convinced himself this was the best way to do it.

Once she'd fallen asleep, he knew what he had to do. No longer would he give up and let Vlad or some operative working for the Company kill him. His new priority was to stay alive, if at all possible, for Mar.

If he had any chance to be with her again, he had to get ready for a war. If things didn't go his way, then at least he'd know he'd gone down fighting.

And he did care about her. He hadn't lied when he told her he'd leave with a heavy heart. His felt like someone had tied a six-hundred-pound anvil to it, and ripped it out of his chest.

All those songs on the radio hadn't lied. Love hurt like hell.

Taking one last look at her, he closed the door silently behind him.

You have to move on.

The walk up the hill wasn't so easy this time. The farther he was away from her, the more his chest tightened. His feet were leaden, and at every step his heart warned him to turn and run back to her.

Come on man, pull it together. You're doing this so that if there is such a thing as miracles, maybe you can be together. He also had the idea that maybe he could draw Vlad's men in a new direction as far away from Mar as possible. He'd felt so bad about deceiving her, but at least he could give her some peace. A chance to live a happy life, without worries about some goon going after her.

It wasn't easy, but he used his mental training to focus on his next moves. First thing he had to do was find a passport guy in Bangkok. The one he'd heard about before he'd run into Mar was dead. But there had to be someone else who could do it for a price. There always was.

As he rounded the back side of the main entrance, he ducked behind a wall. Two of the thugs who'd chased them in Bangkok were checking out his bike.

His body tensed, ready to fight.

Jackson listened as they argued back and forth. One of them instructed the other to check at the desk to see what room Jackson and Mar were in.

The other one called him stupid and said this was a rich hotel. They didn't give away room numbers. Eventually the two decided to sit in their car and wait to see if they could spot their prey.

Jackson needed a new plan.

MAR KNEW AS SOON AS Jackson shut the door that he was gone for good. She'd only pretended to be asleep, knowing that their last lovemaking session was the end. Though she had no plans to stop him, she wanted to know when he left.

Sitting up in bed, she turned on the low lamp. On his pillow Jackson had left her phone and a note.

The phone was dead and she found her charger in her purse and plugged it in. Dreading it, she opened the folded piece of paper he'd left.

Mar,
I care about you, more than I have about anyone else—ever. Sneaking out is a cowardly way to go, but I couldn't stand to see that look in your eyes.

Our last moments together should be happy ones we shared over strawberry pie.

My life is complicated and I didn't lie. While I can't give you details, I can tell you I'm not Mr. Thomas the detective. I sort of walked in on your case accidentally, and decided to help you out. You're going to find all this out as soon as you turn on your phone.

I'm going to do my best to make sure you are safe by creating a diversion. Give me twenty-four hours and then head straight to the airport. Those goons can't get through security so move fast.

Please, understand that I only did what was necessary to survive. I feel guilty as hell keeping things from you, but that's how dire things are for me right now.

That said, I will cherish our time together. You may not believe me, but you stole my heart. I only wish I'd had the courage to tell you to your face.

Jackson

Mar folded the letter back the way it had been.

Tears stung her eyes, then the anger took over.

"Stupid man. I could have helped. Whatever trouble it is." She ranted as she went to the bathroom and washed her face. She'd already decided she couldn't stay here one more minute. This place reeked of Jackson and the longer she stayed the more her heart would break.

"His friggin' life was in danger, and he couldn't tell me." Fists tightening by her sides she resisted the urge to smash them into the mirror.

"I'm mad at myself for falling for a guy I didn't even know." And she had jumped off that cliff and dived in headfirst. "Damn you, Jackson. You made me care again. Then I find out the entire time you were with me was a lie."

Her head ached and her jaw tightened.

Picking up her phone, she saw there were so many messages in her voice mail it could no longer accept more. Rubbing her temples, she sat down on the side of the bed and listened to the first few.

"Mar. Dammit. I've called you five times in the last two hours. Answer your phone," Chi demanded in frustration. "When you get this, you need to get away from that guy you're with because he isn't who he says he is. In fact, he told Mr. Thomas that he was your assistant, so God only knows. He could be an axe murderer. If you don't call me back I'm calling the authorities."

Hitting the button, she skipped through to the end of the messages. It was Chi again. "Thanks for sending the text message. We're glad to know you're alive. I honestly almost called the police and you're going to have several messages at the hotel desk. Can't wait to hear what the deal is with your vacation mate. Call me soon."

Mariska hadn't sent a text message. She scrolled through her outgoing texts. "Oh, my God. The man knows no bounds. How could he do that?" And where were the messages from the front desk? Had he taken care of those, too?

She resisted the urge to toss the phone across the room. Chewing on her lip, she refused to cry.

"Okay. Breathe. You had a fling with a stranger. You

knew that going in. A hot guy with a complicated life, and he was evidently being honest about that part."

Mar thought back to their initial meeting, to what he'd actually said. He'd said he worked all over the world, and that he'd been here researching a few cases. The man had a gift for languages, and he certainly knew how to evade those mob guys in Bangkok.

And he'd solved her case. The anger dissipated a little. He didn't have to help her, but he did. Even put his life in danger to keep her safe.

There was no way she could have found Gladstone on her own. She hadn't even known where to begin searching.

"He knew what he was doing every step of the way. And he helped me. Honestly, he helped me. It's really hard to hate you when I know you're a decent person. Jerk."

And I'm sitting on the bed talking to myself out loud and trying not to cry.

She needed to make sense of it all. If she took her feelings out of it—they'd both been in it for the pleasure. At least that's why she had originally run off with a man she didn't know.

"But why would he come with me?" That was a question she wasn't sure she could answer. He found her attractive. Though he had called her beautiful several times, it went beyond words. She'd seen it in his eyes. There were moments during their time together that she also saw vulnerability in his face, especially when they delved too close to the past.

Whoever Jackson was, he was a good man. She knew that at least.

Mar stared up at the ceiling. As much as she wanted to hate him, she couldn't. Jackson, if that was his name, had given her some of the best days of her life. She'd had fun, and she'd found an intimacy with him that she'd never experienced before.

The phone rang and she nearly fell off the bed, she was so jumpy. "Hello?"

"Mar, what's going on?"

"Hey, Chi, what are you talking about?"

"It's not only me, Makala and Katie are here, too. You're on speaker."

Mar sighed. Katie was a former NYPD detective and had a B.S. detector like no other, and Makala was an FBI profiler and their resident shrink.

"Great. What time is it there? Because you know it's like four in the morning here, right?"

"It's the only time we figured we could reach you. We'll let you get back to bed as soon as you tell us about this new man of yours," Katie insisted. "We demand details. In fact, what kind of guy lies about who he is to get in your pants, and still gets to hang around?"

Blowing out a breath, she thought carefully about what she was about to say. While she doubted she'd ever see him again, she couldn't bring herself to bitch about him. Even though she had every right after what he'd pulled.

"Is he there?" Chi asked. "Go in the bathroom so you can talk to us."

Mar gave a forced chuckle. "No, he's not here. We've parted ways. So he's no longer *my* man." She sniffled. *Damn, I won't cry.*

"Oh, Mar, tell us, hon. What's wrong?" The concern

in Makala's voice was almost her undoing. A tear slid down her cheek, but Mar held it together.

"I'm tired. You know. I had some fun with a mysterious guy. It was the best sex of my life, but he had to leave. End of story."

There was silence on the other end of the phone.

"So you had sex with a guy you'd only known a couple of days?" Chi's statement was one more of admiration than admonishment. "I have to say, I'm kind of proud of you right now. I mean, when you decide to let go, you do it in a big way. But I'm super glad he didn't turn out to be an axe murderer."

Me, too. "I may not be the best detective in the world, you guys, but I do have good sense when it comes to judging people. I still don't know a damn thing about the guy, but my heart tells me he was a good man. Even though he left in the middle of the night and didn't say goodbye."

Again there was silence.

"What? No lectures?" The words came out snappish, but she couldn't help feeling defensive. "You guys are the ones who find fault with every man I meet."

"Did you have a good time?" That was Makala again, but there was no judgment in her voice.

"Uh, you know I did. I can honestly say it was the time of my life. I was happier than I've ever been."

"Well, good for you," Makala said. "There's nothing wrong with stepping out of your comfort zone. You've been through hell this last year and a half. It's okay that you acted out and did something a little wild. We've all been so worried about you."

Mar started giggling. "So you're saying it's a good

thing I had sex with a stranger at a remote island resort, even though I'm not sure I know his name? Have you guys been replaced by pod people?"

They laughed, too.

"Yes, that's what we're saying," Katie teased. "Maka-la's right. You've been so tied up in knots trying to learn the business, and doing a damn fine job I might add, and you haven't even taken the time to process what happened with your mom.

"You took care of your dad and set up his house so that it runs like clockwork. You arranged it so that someone was there to make sure he ate, and that he had clean shirts. By the way, Mrs. Hopkins has been calling with daily updates, and your dad's doing fine. I went over there to make sure, and she made chocolate chip pancakes. The best ones I've ever had. That woman should have a show on the Food Network."

Mrs. Hopkins had been a godsend. Mar's dad was a successful businessman, but he'd taken her mother's death hard. Since Mar was busy trying to keep SIA afloat, she'd hired Mrs. H. to help with the domestic side of things.

Thinking about her dad brought another tear to her eye. *What's with all the crying?* It was like she'd been saving up or something. She reached for a tissue. "Thanks for checking on him. I appreciate it."

"No worries," Katie said. "And Mar, we don't say it enough, but you've kept this place running, too. You're here eighteen hours a day handling research and coor-dinating who does what. We've all had front row seats to the awesomeness that is you."

This time Mar snorted. "I think I need that T-shirt."

"I'll get you one made," Chi said. And she probably would. "So since your dream man is gone, are you coming home?"

Mar chewed on her lip again. "I'm thinking about it. I have to leave here. It feels weird now, but I'm not ready to come home yet. I promise wherever I go, I'll let you know. And from now on I'll keep my phone close by."

"Good girl," Chi said. "Take your time. You don't need to be back until the end of the month."

She was really lucky to have such amazing friends. "Thanks. I heart you guys, you know that, right?"

"Right back at you, chickie," Chi said. "Don't forget to call and let us know where you land."

"I won't," Mar promised.

They said their goodbyes.

"They're right. I needed this. I had a good time, and I met a terrific guy. He lied. A lot. But was fun. So definitely no regrets."

Determined to be strong, she called to arrange for a car to take her back to Bangkok. There was still the danger of the mob guys, so she'd have the driver take her straight to the airport. The shopping would have to wait for another time. The hotel in Bangkok would ship her clothing back to Austin. That way she could travel light, and pick things up as she went.

Once she arrived at the airport, she'd see wherever the next flight was going, and she'd buy a ticket.

Back in the bathroom, she pulled her hair up in a

ponytail, and brushed her teeth. Throwing her toiletries in her backpack as she did.

She followed with her clothes, wadding them into balls and stuffing them in. In less than five minutes she had everything ready to go, and wore her favorite jeans and a T-shirt. The only thing that wouldn't fit was her laptop. She decided she'd have to carry it by hand to the car.

Then she realized it was gone. Jackson had taken her laptop.

And her heart.

Fine. Whatever. I'll buy a new one. I can now add thief to the list of mysterious things about Jackson. Dammit, I never did ask about that tattoo.

Sticking her phone in her hip pocket, she walked to the door. Turning to check the room one last time, she didn't see the intruder, who slapped a hand over her mouth as Mar screamed for her life.

17

SOMEONE HAD GRABBED Mar in the doorway and her fight-or-flight instincts kicked in. Without even thinking about it she shifted her weight, twisted and was about to bring her elbow up to the intruder's chin when she heard, "Mar, it's me. Sorry I startled you. I'm going to take my hand off your mouth now. No one is trying to hurt you. I didn't want you to scream, that's all." Jackson moved his hand away from her mouth.

She stared at him, hard, her heart lodged in her throat. She took a deep breath, and backed away from him. "What are you doing here? I thought you left." It didn't make sense that Jackson stood in her doorway. For the last half hour she'd tried to convince herself that she'd never see him again.

But he was there, the handsome bastard, in his jeans and tight black T-shirt.

I despise him.

Hah. Not hardly.

Mar could take a lot, but the last thing she needed was to face him. The fury from earlier returned. "Did you forget something? Maybe you needed to take my phone, since you already had my *computer?*"

He had the good grace to look ashamed. "I did leave, and I borrowed your computer. I have every intention of returning it to you. That's the absolute truth. But I'm back for a very good reason. Our friends from Bangkok have arrived. I need to get you out of here and on a plane so you'll be safe."

Jackson pushed through the door and shut it.

Mar's hands went to her hips. "Jackson. How do I know this isn't another one of your games? And I'm not going anywhere until you at least tell me your name. I mean it. It pisses me off that I've been calling you Jackson all this time and I don't even know if that's your real name."

She didn't think it possible that she could want someone so much and at the same time be angrier than she'd ever been. To keep from throwing something at him she sat down on the bed and folded her hands on her lap.

"I'm sitting here until you answer my question." Her chin jutted out. "My God. You stole my computer, and who knows what you did to my e-mails. And what about those messages at the front desk? How did you keep those from me?"

The shock on his face was priceless. He hadn't expected her to fight back.

"Mar, there are two men out there who will kill us. We don't have time for explanations." Jackson moved toward her.

"Do not come near me. You are more than welcome to run away again. You did a good job of it an hour ago.

I don't know why you came back or what it is you want now, but I'd prefer if you left immediately."

Liar.

Mar turned away from him and became intensely interested in one of the paintings on the wall. Unlike Jackson, she wasn't a very good liar, but she didn't want him to see that even though he'd betrayed her, she was having a hard time keeping her hands off him.

Stupid jerk. That's right. You're supposed to hate him. He dumped you.

But... No. Don't go there.

"I know you're mad." Jackson lowered his voice and that deep sexy tone was hard to resist. She kept her head turned away. "I understand why, and I'm sorry I deceived you. I promise, whatever I did, it was necessary to protect my cover."

When she continued staring at the wall, he went on.

"My name really is Jackson. It's after one of my mom's favorite soap opera characters. The last name, the one my family gave me, is Walker. I don't use it much, because of the business I'm in. I promise you if you come with me now, I will tell you as much as I can without endangering your life."

Mar turned back around and took in his handsome mug. Something clicked in her brain and she knew he was some kind of intelligence officer. CIA, DEA, something. He was in work mode, and there was a different look about him. His body tensed, as if he were ready for a fight. She'd noticed it when they were at the casino and at the hotel in Bangkok.

He didn't want to blow his cover.

Ding. Ding. Mar won the spy prize.

At the office this past year she'd had a chance to meet with several intelligence officers when the agency consulted on cases with the CIA, FBI and DEA. She knew the way they talked and acted. Even in the boardroom there was a toughness about the agents who actually did field work.

Jackson had that same quiet intensity about him. He was on a mission.

"Good. At least I know the name of the man who made love to me the last three days. So why me, Jackson?" Mar wasn't exactly sure she wanted to hear the answer, but she had to ask.

"What?"

"Why would you come here with me? If you're so worried about blowing your *cover,* and your life is in danger, why spend so much time with me? Seems to me you should be off on some mission somewhere, not making out with a chick on a beach."

He stepped back and leaned against the wall. "I don't know what to tell you." He frowned. "Our meeting was an accident, but I didn't know that until after we arrived here. I thought you were someone else." His arms crossed against his chest and she could tell he told the truth from the confused expression on his face.

"I can't tell you why, but I thought I was supposed to stay close to you. When you mentioned the beach trip, well, at first I thought it was a good idea to get out of Bangkok. But by the time we drove to the resort— I…"

When his voice faltered, she warily gazed up at him. "You what?"

Jackson pushed away from the wall. "I wanted to be with you. I know you don't believe me, but that's the truth." He glanced down at the floor and back up at her. "I understand why you don't exactly feel compelled to come with me right now, but we have to go while it's still dark. I'm telling the truth about the mob guys. I'll take you and show you where they are if you want, but we need to get the hell out of here."

"One more question, then I'll go."

"What?"

"Are you going to hurt me?" She challenged him. Needing to know exactly what his intentions were where she was concerned.

Jackson dropped the hand he'd been about to put on her shoulder, and stepped back. "Mar," he said, his voice strained. "I would give my life for you if necessary. You—are more important to me than anyone else. I promise that all I want to do right now is make sure you are safe. Then you won't ever have to see me again."

Mar believed him. The expression in his eyes told her that he'd been mortified she could even think he would harm her. While she didn't want to admit it, his line about never seeing him again sent a panic through her. She'd lived that reality ten minutes ago and she didn't want to do it again.

The universe had given her a second chance, and she would take advantage of it.

She clicked her tongue on the top of her mouth. "Hopefully it won't be necessary, that whole giving your life for me. Though I'm still kind of pissed at you, so if it comes up, I'm so playing that card. How do you propose we get out of here?"

Jackson stared at her, relief flooding his face when he understood that she would go with him. "Well, they're in the parking lot watching my bike. We're going to have to borrow a car. I'll jack one, but I promise I'll make sure it gets back to the rightful owner." Jackson gave her an earnest look.

Mar rolled her eyes. "Why do you have to make everything so clandestine? How about we use the car I hired? It's picking me up in front of the hotel…" She glanced at her watch. "Right now. Except if those bozos are watching the parking lot that might make it a little tough to get in the car without being seen."

Jackson didn't say anything for a moment. Then he took in her backpack, and the fact that she was already dressed. "You were leaving?"

She pushed past him, and pretended to check something in the bathroom so he couldn't see her face. "Yes. I— I'm bored with this place, and I've decided to spend the rest of my vacation somewhere else. We better go. The car's waiting and those guys are liable to get suspicious if it stays empty," she said.

Mar didn't care about the circumstances that had thrown them together again. She was grateful for more time with the man. She should be furious, but all the anger from before had dissipated. Jackson shouldn't have left her behind, but he'd returned to make sure she was safe. That counted for something in her book.

"Hmm. I think I have an idea." Mar reached for the phone.

The front desk picked up after one ring.

"Hi, I'm hoping you can help me out?"

"We are here to serve, Ms. Stonegate." The gentleman had a French accent.

"Excellent. Listen, my friend noticed some guys who might be paparazzi sitting out in the parking lot. They were checking out his bike and then went back to sit in their car. We're leaving in a few minutes and I would prefer not having my picture flashed all over the tabloids. Um, you know, with my *friend*."

She knew the resort prided itself on being a place where people of certain means could come without worrying about things like paparazzi. The clerk was duly horrified at the prospect of his hotel being invaded by cameras.

"I'll send our security staff immediately to handle the situation. Might I suggest that you meet the car outside the gates? There's an easy path up the beach and through the trees. That way you won't need to worry about them following your car."

Mar explained to Jackson what the clerk had said.

"You never fail to surprise me," he said. "Speaking of that, was that a Krav Manga move you threw at me when I grabbed you in the doorway?"

Mar's right eyebrow lifted. "I keep telling you I can take care of myself. You don't have a former CIA agent for a mother and not pick up a few things here and there. So don't worry. If the bad guys come after you, I've got your back."

Jackson smiled. "I believe you do."

18

THE PLAN WORKED PERFECTLY and Jackson and Mar were in the car on the way to Bangkok with no problems.

Jackson kept an eye on the road behind them. The guys at the hotel weren't stupid. If they'd seen the car pull up and then out again without any guests, they'd get suspicious. Though so far he hadn't seen any sign of them.

Mar's flowery scent teased him. His body urged him to scoop her up in his arms and hold her. Maybe even beg for forgiveness. He couldn't stand the fact that she hated him.

When she asked if he meant her harm, he'd almost come unglued. If he hadn't been worried about her life he would have showed her how much she meant to him right then and there.

He couldn't blame her for being angry about his deception. There was no excuse for what he'd done. He'd taken the coward's way out.

No matter how mad she might be, though, he wouldn't trade those days of heaven with her for anything.

Jackson sensed her movement, and glanced over.

She leaned over to whisper in his ear. "So are you CIA or what?"

Jackson coughed, and studiously ignored her by gazing out the window. *Where the hell had that come from, and how could she possibly know?* Maybe he really was losing his touch.

"No way. You promised me answers." She turned to face him and put her hand on his knee.

Jackson stared down at her fingers. Long and beautiful. Then it dawned on him that she'd touched him. His heart warmed.

"I know you can't tell me everything, but give me the basics," she continued. "You have to work for some government agency. You talked about a cover."

Which was a big slip on his part. That's what had sent her off on this new direction. He knew she wouldn't give up her quest, but it was safer for her if he kept his mouth shut.

"I don't know why I didn't see it before. The way you walk, how careful you are about everything." She eyed him up and down. "Jeez, the way you fold clothes should have told me you were military something. You guys are so precise about everything. Oh, and all those scars on your body. Hello? Big clue."

The scars were a part of his job, so much so that he didn't even see them any more.

"We worked with the DEA on this kidnapping case last summer and those guys, well, they were awesome when it counted, but not the easiest to converse with, if you know what I mean," she said. "And I know you're in trouble. Could you at least tell me the nature of the trouble?"

He chanced a glimpse at her face and wished he hadn't. She seemed so hopeful. After everything he'd done, she still wanted whatever it was between them to work. Jackson didn't have the heart to tell her that it could never happen. There had been weak moments earlier in the evening when he'd believed that he might be able to have a real life with her at some point, but those mob guys reminded him that his life, whatever he had left of it, wouldn't be easy.

Finally he took her hand.

"Mar, I can tell you this. I care about you, and I won't let anything happen to you. Do you understand that? I don't know how long I have to live, but even if it's the last thing I do I'm going to make sure you're safe."

MAR STARED DUMBFOUNDED at Jackson. "How much trouble are you in? What did you do, Jackson?"

Still, he didn't speak. She'd had quite enough of this spy crap. There was a very good chance she could help him, and she wasn't about to give up now.

"Fine. Then we'll play a guessing game." She patted his knee as if he were a child. "You can tell me if I'm warm or cold."

Mar chewed on her lip for a couple of minutes. Then she had an idea. "Let's see. My guess is that you were working on a case and something went wrong. You were probably deep under cover, and it was blown. That's usually what happens in the movies. What I can't figure out is if you're hiding out from the bad guys or your bosses."

When he didn't even acknowledge her, she snapped her fingers. "Or both."

His jaw flinched slightly.

Ding. Ding. Ding.

"Goodness, I am getting really good at this deducing stuff. Okay. Well, I know you're a good guy. Though I'm not sure you think so. Hmm. This is a little tougher." She tucked her tongue into her cheek. "So either someone is framing you or you upset the wrong people and they're out to get you."

At this he swung his head around.

Mar smiled. "Well, what do you know? I seem to have struck a chord. You really need to practice your spy pouting, Jackson. If little ole me can get you to squirm, imagine what those bad guys could do."

She gave him a wicked wink.

Jackson grunted. "They don't have the kind of power over me that you do. I thought you said you were new to the world of investigation. I know operatives who have been in the field for more than twenty years who don't have the deductive reasoning skills you do."

She smiled at that, and the fact that he'd said *operatives* proved her correct.

He held up a hand in surrender. "Damn, if I had a white flag I'd wave it. You're a tough one. Yes. You're on the right path, but I'm not going to give you any more specifics. So please save your psychological torture for someone else."

Mar shrugged. "I'm new to doing it as a job, but like I said before, you don't grow up with a mother like mine without picking up a few things. I also have a Ph.D. in clinical psychology. I may not be as observant as you, but I know human nature. You *are* one of the white hats."

Jackson shook his head. "There's absolutely no way you could know that, Mariska. I'm a dangerous man. I do dangerous work. I lied to you for several days so I could sleep with you. That should say something about the kind of man I am." He scowled.

She made her hands tremble as if she were afraid. "Oohhh, he's the big bad scary Jackson. I'm so frightened." Mar couldn't keep from making fun. "Are you going to show me your scary spy gun, or torture me?"

He harrumphed and turned toward the window again.

She refused to let him think that he was the only one who took advantage of the situation. "And for your information, I used you, too. We were both lonely and needed companionship. We had a wonderful couple of days together. Maybe I didn't know exactly who you were, but I had a good sense of the kind of man you were. Oh, and I read the note. And for the record, I care about you, too."

"Are you finished?" he asked, still facing the window.

"No. I have another question for you. Was it my last name that interested you when we first met?"

He glanced down at the floorboard and then back at her.

Ah. She had hit upon something, though the connection was fuzzy. "You can tell me that much. Did you think I could help you because of my mother?"

He shrugged. "It made me curious. I guess. My

contact told me he had sent help. At the time you seemed to fit the equation, though I couldn't figure out exactly, other than your resources at the office, what it was you were supposed to do for me."

That was part of the reason he'd helped her with Gladstone; he probably thought he was supposed to. Their meeting had been nothing but a lucky coincidence. Mar wasn't complaining.

"I didn't know your mom," Jackson interrupted her thoughts, "but I knew of her. I did use your computer a couple of times. Your IP is untraceable and that's something I desperately needed. That's why I took it with me."

Knowing that he used her for her computer didn't really bother her like it should. He'd been in a desperate situation. She might have done the same in his shoes.

"Huh. Okay. So you sent superspy messages out, and you were hiding away with me until you received answers. So, someone must have finally contacted you. And that's why you left."

"Mariska," he said her name sharply. "I can't answer your questions. I'm sorry, but that's the way it is. I'm taking you straight to the airport and then we're done. Do you understand?"

"Oh, sure, Jackson. But I can tell you right now being an ass isn't going to work with me. While I'm not exactly over you being so deceptive, I have this great capacity for understanding why."

He ignored her.

Frustrated, she threw up her hands. "Do you have any idea what it is I see in you? Really? You gave me some of the happiest days of my life. And made love to me so many times I lost count. It wasn't just sex. I know the difference, and so do you." She tugged on his sleeve to get his attention.

"Then there's that letter. You came out and said it. You care about me. You've said it a dozen times in the last hour. Was that a lie? Can you at least tell me that much?"

Jackson gawked at her as if she were insane. "No."

"No what, Jackson?"

He crossed his arms and she knew it was one of his defenses. He had a hard time keeping his hands off her, even though he was perturbed with her. "No, it wasn't a lie."

That was all she needed to hear.

Mar grabbed both of his hands in hers. She saw the flicker of need in his eyes when she touched him. He really was like a wild mustang who needed taming, but she needed the right approach.

"Do you understand how much I care about you? That I would do anything for you, Jackson?"

He crossed his arms against his chest. "You don't know me. You know parts of me, Mariska, but you don't know what I'm capable of and you can't help me."

Mar kissed him. At first he kept his mouth tight, until she used her teeth to nip at his lips. His mouth opened and he kissed her back.

She really could lose herself in the man.

He groaned as he lifted his head away from her. He gently pushed her back to her side of the car. "We can't do this. The people who are after me are more dangerous than those guys back at the hotel," he warned her. "I'd given up before I met you. I can tell you this. I would give anything to be with you, but it isn't possible."

That was all she needed to hear. He wanted to be with her. What Jackson didn't know is that she was the grand facilitator of problem fixing. The past year, she'd discovered that she could tackle most anything if she broke it down into small steps.

What Jackson needed was a way out of his trouble. She would do whatever it took to make that happen.

"Come with me now, Jackson. We'll get on a plane and be back in the States tomorrow. I know how this sounds, but I know people, Jackson. We can help you."

"Mar, I can't jump on a commercial flight. Interpol will be all over me. Once that happens I'll disappear. That's what happens to people like me. It's one of the reasons they call us ghosts. One minute we're there, the next we're gone, and no one cares."

"I care." Mar tapped her finger on his thigh as she thought. "If we can get you home to the States can you clear up the problem with your bosses?"

Jackson put his hand on hers to stop the tapping. "Please. Let me do this my way. Go to the airport and get on a plane. If I know you're safe, it'll make everything so much easier."

Mariska had a network of family and friends that could make almost anything possible. And if that didn't work there were always Chi's friends. Something snapped in Mar's tired brain and she realized Chi was the answer.

Mar held up a hand. "You're really cute when you're worried. Hold that thought."

She picked up her phone and remembered the battery was almost dead. She didn't have enough juice to make one call. "Hey, do you have a phone I can borrow? I need to call home and let them know I'm coming."

Jackson handed her his phone. It was one of those you bought on the street with a certain amount of minutes. Then you tossed it when you were done.

"That's so Jason Bourne."

"What?" He was thoroughly perplexed.

"You know, in the movies he always has these phones so they can't be traced?" She tried to explain.

"I have no idea who you are talking about. Are they recent movies?"

Jackson acted like he didn't know who Jason Bourne was? "Are you kidding me, you haven't seen those movies? My God, Jackson, what kind of hole do they keep you in?" She waved her hand. "Don't answer that. Anyway, it's funny that you're like this superspy guy because when I first saw you I thought you were Matt Damon, and he plays that role."

"Sorry. I've never heard of him," Jackson said as he shrugged. "I don't have much time to get out and see movies."

"Whatever." Mariska grinned. The guy must have been a real twenty-four-hour-a-day spy not to have gone to the movies in the last ten years. Feeling sorry for him, she decided she'd have to fix that at the first opportunity.

Well, he wasn't the only one who had tricks up his sleeve. Picking up the phone, she dialed Chi's number.

19

THE CAR STOPPED AND Mar glanced up from the phone to see why. She watched while a man tried to shepherd a cow and several pigs across the road. He wasn't very successful, and it appeared they might be there awhile.

When Jackson opened the door, she thought he was going to help the guy with the cow, but he turned and went the opposite direction. There was a black sedan behind them. Two men jumped out with guns.

A shot rang out. Instinct had her ducking behind the seat. But worry about Jackson made her raise her eyes up so she could peek out. As she did, she watched as he kicked the gun out of one man's hand while twisting and turning so that the other one missed a punch.

The punch landed on the man's partner, and he stumbled back, giving Jackson enough room to pop each of his knees with wicked kicks. Mar grimaced and could almost feel the bones breaking as the man went down.

Jackson turned his attention to the last one standing,

and threw an elbow into the man's neck. Then punched him solidly in the nose, blood spurting out.

It was horrific and mesmerizing at the same time, and it all happened so fast she didn't have time to respond. Jackson anticipated every move, and it was like watching an action film, except the man she loved was the extreme bone cruncher.

Wow.

The man he'd hit in the face fell forward. The other one writhed in pain. He wouldn't be walking anytime soon.

Jackson patted them both down searching for more weapons, and picked up their guns along with some knives. Opening the door, he threw the weapons in the front seat with their driver. Then he grabbed his backpack.

"Are you— What the? What are you doing?" she stuttered, confused.

"Getting some rope." He reached into his backpack.

The absurdity of the situation caught up with her. "You carry rope in your backpack?"

Jackson wiped some sweat off his brow. "Sure."

Then he shut the door.

Mar opened it, but she stopped when Jackson turned toward her and pointed a finger. "Get back in there. It still isn't safe."

She started to argue she could handle herself, but stopped when the man who fell down last tried to get back up. Jackson slammed his face into the hood of the car again. He didn't move after that.

Mar winced and returned to the car.

"Fine, I'll wait in here." Her superspy was a cut-throat assassin. "I'm really glad he's on my side," she whispered to no one in particular.

Jackson tied the rope around the men and then dragged them to the back of the car. She couldn't see what was happening, but the trunk lid popped open. Then he shut it and hopped in the driver's seat. Mar couldn't for the life of her figure out what he was doing until he pulled the vehicle off into the field to the right.

After that, he jumped out of the car and walked over to the shepherd, handing him several bills. Then he climbed back in the car.

"It's getting warm out there," he said as he bent over and closed up his bag.

Mar started laughing, somewhat hysterically. "Seriously." She sputtered. "After all that, you're going to talk about the weather? Are you okay? Did they hurt you?"

He shrugged. "We had a problem and I took care of it." His face was a total blank, as if he did that sort of thing every day.

Hell, maybe he did.

"Why did you jump out of the car like that? They had guns and could have killed you," Mar chastised.

"I had the element of surprise in my favor, and they didn't kill me. I'm fine."

"Yes, but…"

"Mar, I handled the situation." He gave her an end-of-discussion stare.

She rolled her eyes. "Not that I care, but are they still alive?"

"They won't be waking up any time soon, but I didn't kill them. The shepherd will wait until this evening to call the authorities and report the car running off the road. That should give us enough time to get you to the airport."

She wasn't going anywhere without Jackson. "Uh, no. I'm still calling my friend. Let's see what she has to say and then I'll consider your offer to go to the—"

Jackson cleared his throat. "Mar, I'm not taking no for an answer. You saw those guys. There will be more of them when those two don't report in. We have to get you out of here."

The man was so hardheaded. "Hey," she said, frustration edging her voice. "I'm asking you to give me a chance. I saw what you can do, Jackson. You are friggin' scary amazing. But give me a chance to show what I can do. I know you don't have a lot of faith in my abilities, but I promise you I can help."

Then she leaned across the seat and threw her arms around him, truly happy he was safe. "I'm so glad you're okay. And the fact that you are total badass is making me kinda hot."

He hugged her back. "You're trying to distract me, aren't you?"

She squeezed him tighter. "Maybe."

He kissed her, then said against her lips, "It's working. And for the record, I have no doubt about your abilities, but these are extreme circumstances."

"But you're going to let me try, aren't you?" she asked him.

Jackson closed his eyes briefly and then glanced back at her. "Yes."

IF MARISKA WANTED CHI'S help, she had to do some fast talking. The other woman didn't like doing anything that wasn't within the confines of the law, though Chi was also the queen of loopholes. She took a few minutes to gather her thoughts.

The driver had started the car again, and was discussing the route with Jackson.

She picked up Jackson's phone from the floorboard where she'd dropped it when the gunshot blasted.

Dialing Chi's number, she hoped the other woman would pick up.

"Hello." Her friend's voice was hesitant.

"Hey, it's me," Mar said.

"Mar, whose phone are you on?" Chi's tone was cautious.

"It's Jackson's secret spy phone." She snorted at that.

She heard him groan, and glanced up to see him rolling his eyes.

Chi asked, "Jackson? Did you chase him down with your car or something? Last time we talked, which was, um, a little over an hour and a half ago, you said he ran away and was gone for good."

"Well, he came back to save me from some mob guys." Mar still hadn't thanked him for that.

"What the hell are you talking about?" Chi wasn't pleased. "When did you get mixed up with the mob? Are you okay?"

Oops. "I'm fine. The mob thing happened when I searched for Gladstone. I promise to explain every detail later, but right now we're in a bit of a hurry and I really need you to do some of your special magic."

Mar chose her words carefully. Everything depended on Chi understanding how important this was. "We need a way to get us out of the country without Interpol crawling all over our asses. Jackson can't travel through the normal channels but we have to get him back to the States. His life depends on it."

Silence.

"Please?" Mar begged.

"Uh. That's pretty heavy stuff there, Mar," Chi warned. "I mean if he's in so much trouble that Interpol is after him. Come on. You need to run in the other direction."

Mar was determined to make her comprehend the gravity of the situation and why she couldn't leave Jackson alone. "Chi, that's not going to happen. I know how it sounds, but I need you to do this for me."

"Are you in love with this guy?" Chi sounded like she already knew the answer.

There was a long pause as Mar thought about it. What she had with Jackson was much more than lust or a vacation fling. In the short time they'd been together, she'd fallen for him in a big way. Even with all the deception, she wanted to spend the rest of her life with the man.

"Your silence speaks volumes." Chi sighed. "This is a lot of trouble for someone you met only a few days ago."

Mar stared at the man in the seat next to her. "I know, but he's definitely worth it." He pretended as though he wasn't listening. Mar noticed a slight cut above his brow. Holding the phone between her shoulder and her ear, she searched her bag for a tissue and some of the antiseptic she always carried. "Please, Chi. I need your help."

"All right." Chi didn't sound completely convinced it was a good idea, but Mar knew she would come through for her. "I'll call in some favors. Tell him I need to know who he works for, because I have to go directly to the source if we're going to make this happen."

Holding her hand over the phone, Mar asked, "Um, so are you CIA? Chi needs to know for sure."

He refused to answer.

"Jackson, please. At least let me try to help. It hurts my heart to think something horrible could happen to you if we don't get you home. I'm good at this sort of thing, let me do this for you."

"CIA," he said with a clipped tone.

Jeez, it wasn't like she hadn't figured it out for herself. She only needed confirmation. "CIA," she repeated.

Chi blew out a breath. "Okay. Randy is the deputy director there. I don't suppose your friend will share what happened?"

Mar knew better than to even ask Jackson. No way would he reveal any more than he had. "No. Tell them that he's willing to turn himself in, but we have to get him home. That isn't easy since there's been some kind of big misunderstanding. There are people out there who are trying to kill him."

"Okay," Chi told her, "listen carefully. This is going to take me a bit. I've pulled a lot of strings in my lifetime, but nothing like this. Is there some place you can hole up, and I'll call you back as soon as I know something?"

Mar shouldn't feel relieved, but she did. At least if

Chi was on their side they had a chance. Once she gave her word, her friend would do anything to make it happen. "Sure. We'll take in the sights for a few hours. And Chi, I really appreciate this."

"No worries. Though I can't promise you anything."

She hung up.

Now Mar had to convince Jackson that they needed a little more time before heading to the airport.

She explained what Chi had told her.

Jackson gave her a look of incredulity. "Mar, it doesn't work like that. Your friend can't call up the deputy director and ask for a free pass. I've been disavowed. I no longer exist in their eyes. Why can't you understand that? This isn't some case your agency can tie up in a few days. And trust me, the real life of someone like me isn't fodder for some action movie." He slumped against the window.

She knew he wouldn't believe any platitudes, so she spoke from her heart. "I understand better than you think. I read some of my mom's journals. While she was never very specific about details, there was enough there to know that her life had been in danger more than once."

That wasn't a lie. Mar had been shocked when she read some of the events from her mother's past. If anything, it made her respect her even more. It certainly explained why her mother had always been so firm about Mar improving her mind and insisting her daughter be able to protect herself physically.

"All I'm asking is that you give Chi a few hours to see what she can do," Mar said. "When I tell you she is a magician, I'm not lying. Client privilege keeps me from divulging too much, but the woman has worked miracles in the past."

Jackson glanced at her again. He took a deep breath. "Every minute we stay in this country puts both our lives in more danger, not only from the mob, but also from the people who were after me before we ever met. I need you to go to the airport and get on a plane. That's the best thing you can do for both of us. Please."

He was so earnest.

"I will. I promise you, Jackson. I will do whatever you ask. But you have to give Chi four hours. If she can't find a way to help you, then I promise you can drive me straight to the airport and I won't say another word."

She gave him a reassuring smile and turned to the driver and tapped on the glass. The window separating their seats rolled down and she leaned forward.

"Sir, we aren't quite ready to go to the airport yet." She dug through her purse and pulled out a piece of paper with a picture on it. "Can you take us here." She pointed to the Wat Chalong and Phuket Temple. She'd planned to check out the historic site and she didn't think the Thai mob or assassins after Jackson would be hanging out there.

She pulled three hundred dollars out of her purse. "And I need you to sort of hang around and wait for us if you don't mind. It may be a few hours."

20

"THAT IS ONE BIG BUDDHA," Mar exclaimed nervously as they entered Wat Phra Thong.

Jackson couldn't believe he had let her rope him into this sightseeing tour. *I've really lost my mind.* Their lives were in imminent danger and he was walking around a temple with her.

"The reason you only see the top half is they can't dig the rest of it up. Everyone who tries to do it ends up cursed. It's solid gold. Amazing. Don't you think it's incredible?" As a tour guide she wasn't half-bad.

He could tell she was worried, too, even though she acted like running for her life was an everyday occurrence. He'd noticed how she cased the room and watched people, even while she took in the sights.

At least some of what he'd tried to teach her had rubbed off. He had to admit since it was a Monday the place wasn't very crowded, so it was easier to keep an eye on the surroundings.

"Jackson, there's something I need to talk to you about." She motioned him over to a nearby plaque away from the crowds. "I know you're going through a lot of crap right now, and there's a good chance you may be, um, tied up for some time. But I was wondering—" Mar stumbled over the words.

"At this point, you can ask me anything, except about what's going on with the Company." Jackson put a hand on her shoulder. "Are you wondering if we have a possibility of a future?" He knew they'd have to talk about it eventually. And their time together grew shorter by the minute.

Mar moved so that she could slide under his arms and put her hands around his waist. "It's not fair to even ask. In my head I know that. You have no idea if they'll believe you or what will happen even if they do. I could kill whoever it was who caused all this trouble."

"You'd have to stand in line for that," Jackson grumbled. "I don't know what to tell you, Mar. Do I want a future that includes you. Yes. I'm having a hard time trying to think of my world without you in it. They say when you find the right one, it can happen fast. I never believed that until now.

"But, and I can't say this enough, my future is bleak at best right now. I'm wanted for treason for crimes against the United States. There's a lot that has to happen in order to make that go away. I don't feel right making you promises I may not be able to keep." He pulled her tighter. "It kills me to say those words."

Mar nodded, blinking back the tears that threatened to fall. The sight of those tears was almost his undoing. But he saw as she straightened herself and cleared her throat. "You know I seem to remember someone saying every relationship has its problems."

That was his girl. She was trying to be strong for

him. Jackson chuckled, but it wasn't a happy sound. "I need you to make me a promise, Mar." He paused while another couple walked by. He took another quick glance around to make sure no one was taking an interest in them.

"What?" Mar gave him a wary look.

"You have to keep moving forward." He said the words carefully, as if he wanted her to understand the underlying meaning. "You can't do what you've done this past year and a half after your mom died. You have to live your life and be happy." He took her hands in his and rubbed his fingers over hers. "I need to know that whatever happens you are happy."

Mar took a deep breath. It wasn't a promise she could make to him, no matter how hard she wanted to. A future without Jackson was nothing but disappointment. She knew that with all of her heart. "I will try." She leaned up and kissed his cheek.

The driver had charged Mar's phone while they were touring the temple, and he handed it to her, before pulling out onto the street. She checked it now and Jackson saw the disappointment on her face when there weren't any new calls.

He wasn't surprised. This pipe dream of hers was nothing short of crazy, but he felt compelled to give her a few more hours. Selfish bastard. If he were honest he was giving himself a few more hours with her. He could have insisted they go straight to the airport.

Her phone rang and she jumped and dropped it.

Scooping it up, he handed it to her.

"Chi?" It was Mar's friend, probably calling to tell her she was sorry, but nothing could be done.

Mar was silent for a bit. "Really? I— Chi. Thank you." Relief washed over her face and Jackson didn't know what to think.

She handed the phone to him. "Um, the deputy director would like to speak to you."

Jackson's breath caught. It couldn't be. Once agents had been disavowed, the Company had nothing to do with them. Jackson had scum-sucking Dawson to thank for that.

He put the receiver against his ear.

The phone was silent for a few minutes then Chi came back on. "Deputy Director, I have Jackson on the line with us."

"Sir, this is Jackson Walker." His voice faltered a bit, and he took a breath to steady his nerves. Though his stomach was tied in a hard knot, and didn't seem to get the message his brain sent.

"Son, you're in a boatload of trouble." The deputy director was known for being a direct, no-B.S. kind of guy, which was something out of the ordinary in their business.

Jackson took a steadying breath. "Yes, sir, I know." It really was him.

"We decoded the ad in the *Times*. That was from you, right?"

"Yes, sir. It was. I want to come in."

"Do you understand the charges that will be brought against you for treason?" The man sounded dire, but Jackson was prepared.

As an agent he knew the rules going in, but the alternative was death. He'd take whatever they threw at him. "Yes, sir. I'd like the opportunity to tell the truth and that's all I'm asking. I think there may have been some confusion, and I believe I have information that would be beneficial to the Company. Intel that could shed light on my situation as well as save some lives."

There was silence on the other end. So he continued. "It's always been my plan to turn myself in, sir." If something happened between this call and him making it back to Langley he wanted the deputy director to know that it had never been his intention to go off the grid.

"Then why did you run?" The other man was good at what he did and there was no emotion behind his voice.

"Sir, you and I both know this line isn't secure. But I had no choice. At least I thought I didn't, since the Company blacklisted me."

"What the hell are you talking about?" the deputy director demanded.

"My handler said I'd been disavowed and accused of treason. That's why I went off the grid."

"I see," the deputy director said. "We have a great deal to discuss. We've already arranged for transport. You'll be made aware of the arrangements in a few moments."

"Yes, sir. Thank you."

There was silence on the other end.

"Jackson, are you there?" Chi asked.

He had to clear his throat before he spoke to her, emotion weighing down his vocal cords. He had a chance. "Yes, I'm here," he said. "I don't know how the hell you did that, but thank you." Mar's friend really was a miracle worker. In fact, Jackson was already wondering if maybe he was in a dream and that the conversation with the deputy director was a part of it.

She grunted. "It wasn't easy. Luckily I have some history with his family or I doubt he would have taken my call, though when I told him that you were involved he suddenly became very interested."

"I bet he did."

"How's my girl doing? Are you keeping her away from those mobsters?"

"Absolutely. Nothing is more important to me right now than her safety. I wish you'd convince her to get on a plane."

Mar slapped at his arm and tried to pull the phone away. He held up a hand.

"Until she knows you're safe, she wouldn't listen to the Pope. But I think we have— Hold on a second. The deputy director is finalizing the plans. Give me a minute."

He could hear Chi talking on another phone, but not what she was saying. His mind reeled from the fact that he'd had a discussion with the deputy director. There were agents who had entire careers without ever speaking to the man.

A second later she came back on the line.

"Okay, a military transport plane is going to meet you at the Phuket airfield. Wherever you guys are, you need to head there directly. Lt. Colonel Scott Owen will be there to meet you in about an hour. I can't tell you how lucky we are with that one. He happened to be there doing military training on new systems hardware.

"The transport has to make some stops, but you two will stay on that plane until you reach Virginia, where the lieutenant colonel and the deputy director will escort you to Langley."

"Okay," Jackson said unbelievingly. He had a ride home, and Mar would be safe. It was too much. This wasn't the way his life usually went.

"Listen," Chi said, "it's going to be tough on Mar, to watch you walk away in handcuffs. I'm arranging it so that she is taken off the plane first when it reaches Virginia. Then I've hired a private jet to bring her back here. She cares about you, and you better make this as easy as possible for her. Do you understand me?"

He couldn't help but smile. He liked that her friends were so protective. "Loud and clear. For the record, there's nothing I want more than for her to be happy."

"I have a feeling it's going to be a while before that happens. It kills me that she's fallen for a guy she may never see again."

Jackson gazed into Mariska's beautiful green eyes. "I'm going to do my best to make sure that doesn't happen."

"As long as we understand each other."

"We do."

"Good."

He could have been offended by Chi's words, but he understood exactly what she meant. Letting go of Mariska would be the hardest thing he'd ever done, but he'd make it as easy on her as possible, and he'd fight to be back in her life if he was ever able to clean up the mess he was in.

"I still can't believe you did all this in a few hours. I've been trying to get home for two months, and I'm a trained operative."

Chi laughed. "You should see what I can do when I haven't just run six miles on the treadmill. Be safe, and take care of our girl."

He hung up.

"It can't be that easy." Jackson stared at the phone. "I mean. I had a conversation with the deputy director. That doesn't happen. Do you understand what I'm talking about?"

Mar gave him the sweetest smile.

"I told you I know people. Well, technically in your case, I know people who know people. I can't promise that it'll be daisies, but at least you'll have a chance to plead your case, or whatever it is you guys do."

She really was his angel. He didn't know how or why they met in that bar, but he would be forever grateful.

"And for the record, Jackson," she said. "I would do anything for you. Hurry up and get this mess straightened out. I can't wait to introduce you to Mississippi mud pie, peach cobbler and my personal favorite, cherry chocolate cake, with a creamy center."

Jackson pulled her into his lap and hugged her.

"Baby, I have no idea what the future holds, but you're all the dessert I'll ever need." He didn't know if he would ever see her again, but he would remember the sight, smell and touch of her for whatever life he had left.

21

Two months later

MAR SAT AT HER DESK at the SIA and wondered if there would ever be a day when she didn't think of Jackson. It had been two months since he'd kissed her on the military transport and then she'd been forced to walk away from him.

Her stomach still fluttered when she thought about that kiss and his last words to her. "You're my reason for living. No matter what happens I'll never stop thinking about you." The way he'd said the words had seemed so ominous and final. As if he believed he would never see her again.

She'd refused to believe it. Each morning she opened her eyes and prayed it would be the day Jackson walked back into her life. But so much time had passed she wondered if it would ever happen. If he wasn't able to prove his innocence he could be spending the rest of his life in prison.

Mar's heart was heavy with anxiety.

She and Chi had tried to get information about what

happened to him once he walked off the plane, but it was classified, and the deputy director wasn't talking. He told Chi it was an ongoing investigation, and there would be no discussing it with her.

Mar had thrown herself into her work. While she had put in long hours before her time in Thailand, now she only went home to sleep a few hours and change clothes. The cases kept her mind busy so she couldn't think of those steamy nights on the beach with the man of her dreams.

The man she loved. She could kick herself. If only she'd told him before they parted. Even if they never saw each other again, at least he would know he was loved.

But she decided this morning that she had to put the past behind her. Jackson may not have felt the same way about her. Oh, he cared, she knew that, but there was no telling what they'd done to him. If he survived he might not even want to remember her.

If by some miracle he had been able to clear his name then there was a good chance he was working somewhere else in the world. If she were Jackson, she'd want a fresh start.

She deserved that, too. To get her mind on happier things, she'd planned to take the weekend off and do a little self-nurturing. Shopping, lying on the couch watching marathons of *Doctor Who*. Whatever her tired, sad heart desired.

"Hey, chica, we're heading down to the Tapas Bar for some drinks and eats," Katie interrupted Mar's thoughts. "Chi says you're going whether you want to or not. It's two-for-one margaritas and wine night."

Mar waved a hand over her desk. "It's Friday and I have to get these files cleaned up so I can take off this weekend."

Katie's hands went to her hips. She might only be five foot two and a hundred pounds, but Katie was a woman to be reckoned with. She'd survived three years as an NYPD detective, so she was a lot tougher than she appeared. "We'll have none of that." She wagged a finger. "Mar, you know those files will be here on Monday. You need to relax and have a few drinks with your friends who love you. Chi and I will drag you by force, or you can come on your own. Oh, and Makala is back in town, so the whole gang is going to be there."

It had been a long time since she'd gone out with her friends. They'd all given her a wide berth while she dealt with her emotions surrounding the situation with Jackson. Still, she had a ton of work. "I don't know."

"You're the boss. You know how important it is to be friendly with the employees and inspire goodwill. And, um, buy the first round."

Mar laughed. The cases could wait, and she really could use a drink. Listening to her friends talking about their lives might be the perfect thing to pull her out of her own head.

Stepping around her desk, Mar smiled. She was lucky to have such wonderful people around her. They deserved some fun, and so did she. Besides, she could clean up her desk later.

"DID YOU HEAR THAT Katie made out with that cute DEA Agent Cruz?" Patience wagged her eyebrows.

The eight main players from the office sat around a

large round table at the Tapas Bar. As they sipped wine, they tasted a variety of delicacies from dolma to Mar's personal favorite, feta stuffed olives.

Thankfully, there weren't any desserts. Sweets reminded her of Jackson and she was determined not to think about him tonight.

Mar tried to pay attention to the banter between her friends. They'd been so great when she'd gathered them all in the conference room her first day back in the office. After everything that had happened with Jackson, Mar could no longer live with the lies in her life.

Chi, Katie and Makala had been there for support when she told the rest of the group the truth that while she was her mother's daughter, she was far from the top investigator everyone expected her to be.

The big surprise surprised no one. They'd gone along with the ruse because they could see how hard she was trying to make it work. The funny thing was, they actually valued the contributions she did make. Patience, their forensic anthropologist, was the one who spoke up first and said Mar had saved her tons of research time, so that she could spend more hours in the field. After that, they all chimed in.

The meeting had ended with Mar in happy tears. Terribly unprofessional, but her friends didn't seem to care. Since meeting Jackson, tears seemed to come more easily to her.

"We were on a job," Katie ground out between gritted teeth, defending her kiss with Cruz. "In a club, dancing. Trying to fit in. Hello, I'm the chick who found the creep who had our hostage, remember?"

Mar patted her arm. "Yes, you are the big hero."

She blew her a kiss. "But I am curious, was he any good?"

They all chuckled at that.

The wine had helped her relax. She'd been so tied up in knots for so long. It felt good to get out among the living again.

Chi seemed unusually quiet. She kept checking her phone. Mar leaned over and nudged her shoulder. "You doing okay? You seem kind of tired tonight."

The other woman smiled. "I'm still jet-lagged from London yesterday. I must be getting old because those forty-eight-hour turnarounds used to be a breeze for me."

"Yeah, that's what I think of when I look at that amazing olive skin and perfect bod—she's old," she joked with her.

They both laughed.

Chi put an arm around Mar's shoulder. "It's good to see you eating again. I've been worried we might have to do some kind of anorexia intervention."

Mar blew air out her lips. "As if." *Stop it. That's the past. I decided today that I'm moving on.*

"I guess maybe I haven't been on my regular routine, but I've suddenly decided I'm hungry, so bring on the grub." She stuffed a dolma in her mouth to prove her point, and winked at her friend.

"Huh. Well, it's good to see you have your appetite. You're going to need all of your strength," Chi said under her breath.

Mar swallowed so fast she almost choked. "Why? Did you hear something?"

Chi gave her a mysterious look. "No. I told you it

could be six months to who knows when. Wasn't talking about that." That was something they'd agreed not to discuss after Mar had told her friend everything over two bottles of wine and a cryfest to end all cryfests. "I was talking about work. You've helped bring in so much business the past couple of months. You need to keep your strength up. That's all."

Mar sighed again. "Oh. I thought. Never mind."

She straightened and pushed thoughts of Jackson away. "I think I may eat my weight in olives tonight." Mar reached for an olive and stuffed it in her mouth. And tried not to think about how creative Jackson could be with the dishes before her.

22

JACKSON WATCHED FROM the doorway of Mar's office. A foot of case files stacked on her desk, she was intently studying each one. She hadn't noticed him yet. He'd really have to work on that. Almost ten o'clock on a Friday night and she was hard at it. He'd have to do something about that, too.

The office reflected her personality. Classy but comfortable, with dark woods and light cream walls. She had her hair tied up in a clip and she looked every bit as gorgeous as he remembered.

When she scrunched her shoulders to her ears, Jackson couldn't help but laugh.

The noise made her jump and she almost fell out of her chair.

"You know, there's a great place in Bangkok where you can get a massage." Jackson grinned as she ran across the room, bumping her knee on a table as she did. Then she flung herself at him.

"Oh, my God. I didn't think you were ever going to get out of that place," she screamed happily.

Jackson squeezed her tight to him, taking in that

luscious flowery smell that was Mar. "Me, either," he whispered before capturing her lips in his.

He reluctantly lifted his head so he could see her face again. No, she was really there and she was holding on to him for dear life. It wasn't a dream. He'd thought about this moment so many times, but nothing came close to the real thing.

Squeezing her tight again, he told her, "I'm here now. Sorry it took so long."

She pushed away, giving him the once-over. "You look good. I was afraid they'd beat you or something. I bet you need to eat, did they feed you?"

Jackson laughed again and picked her up in his arms. Swinging her around. "I missed you." This time he assailed her mouth, savoring every inch of it.

When he lifted his head, she let out a happy sigh. "I missed you, too. Come and sit down. I know from Chi that you can't tell me what happened, but at least tell me you don't have to go back."

Jackson pulled her onto his lap. "Do you really want to discuss all that now?"

She nodded. "I need to know, whatever you can tell."

"Well, ninety-nine percent of it is classified, but I can tell you this. I was set up, by someone I thought was a friend." Dawson in London had compromised Jackson with Vlad in hopes of making his own arms deal. It was Dawson who wrote the burn notice and dumped Jackson in Thailand.

The truth was, Jackson had never been burned. When he'd contacted Dawson, who was his handler, the notice had been confirmed. Dawson had told him to jump the grid and to stay off it. He'd help when he could. Jackson had been an idiot and believed him.

What he'd learned over the past two months was Dawson had faked evidence indicating Jackson was a part of some sleeper cell in Eastern Europe. He'd been branded a traitor by the United States government, and that was why the execution order had been sent out on him. It had taken Jackson over a month to explain the details of what had really happened. Once they knew the truth, the Company was able to piece together information that proved it was Dawson who had been part of the sleeper cell.

"My saving grace was that someone else—" his friend Pete who had e-mailed him about the trap "—was on to what was happening. He and his handler were the ones who convinced Langley that it was all one big mess."

Jackson had gone through almost a month of questioning about why he didn't follow protocol. The only things that had helped him make it through were that he had the truth on his side, and that eventually he'd find Mar waiting for him. At least he'd hoped she would wait. He refused to let himself think otherwise.

He hadn't been allowed to work the operation that took Dawson down, but he'd watched from headquarters. His former handler was no longer a threat. Jackson's only regret was that he wished he could have been the one to bring him in. The man had nearly ruined his life, and he'd put the woman Jackson had come to love in danger. That was his most unforgivable sin.

Still, the irony that he might have never met Mariska if he hadn't been in trouble wasn't lost on him.

"So do you still work for them?" Her voice was soft with worry.

"No. Once everything was cleared up, I retired. But don't worry. I'll start my job search on Monday." He had benefits, and he'd socked away almost all of his salary from the last eight years. He could well and truly retire if he wanted, but he knew he needed more.

She pursed her lips together. "Good. I can't even imagine how I'd feel every time you'd have to go off on some crazy mission. I looked up that tattoo on your neck, I know the skull and the number have to do with how many times you've been shot and lived. I'd really rather that number not go any higher."

Jackson couldn't agree more. "Don't worry. I'll get a job protecting poodles or something inane like that. No more spy stuff."

She snorted. "Poodles? Forget that. You don't need to search for work. You can join the SIA. Oh, my God. You'd be perfect," she said in a rush of excitement, "and it's about time we had a man on staff. We could use some testosterone around here."

Jackson enjoyed her enthusiasm and her willingness to help. "That's sweet of you, but I'm not big on hand-outs." No, he'd find a job in security. He wasn't really worried, and he'd try to find something here in Texas, though he'd probably make more money in New York or London.

"There's nothing sweet about it. You know about the staff here. My mom set it up so we have the best investigators in the business. We do a lot of international work. Hell, your gift for languages alone could save us a lot of time. Yesterday I was trying to deal with a man who only spoke Portuguese, and I really could have used your help. How many languages do you speak, exactly?"

Jackson had to stop and think. "In all I probably have a working knowledge of about thirty, but I'm fluent in about fifteen."

"See, there you have it."

Jackson squeezed her to him. "You are so beautiful."

"Stop it." She swatted at him. "I want you to take this seriously. At least tell me you'll consider it, and that you'll come in and talk to the rest of my gang? They're all dying to meet you."

"I'll consider it, but the reason I'm here isn't for a job. I want to take you out on a proper date, dinner, maybe a movie? You'll have to pick the film, I'm not sure what's in the theater these days." He'd been so busy trying to clear his name that he hadn't paid much attention to the rest of the world the last few months.

"Hmm. A proper date, where you take me to the porch and kiss me good-night?"

"Exactly." They'd started their relationship in a very heated way, and Jackson planned to take some time to court her. He'd go the old-fashioned route for once. It was the first time in his life he'd even allowed himself to think about a long-term relationship and he wanted to do it right.

Mar really had become his sole reason for living the past few months, and he was going to do whatever he could to convince her to spend the rest of her life with him.

Mar pursed her lips. "Uh, I don't think so."

Her answer caught him by surprise. Then it dawned on him, she probably had other plans. What an idiot he'd been. It was Friday night. The idea that she might have a date with another man hit him hard, leaving him feeling like he'd been punched in the gut.

She grabbed his face between her hands. "Stop, whatever it is you're thinking. I can see those wheels turning in your head. Of course I want to go on a date with you."

Jackson laughed with her. "I thought maybe you were seeing someone else."

Mar joked, "For such a smart guy you can be so crazy sometimes. Jackson, I've been waiting months for you to get out of that place, and then you think I could even look at another man? What is wrong with you?"

He loved it when she had that sparkle in her eyes. That she was mad pretty much made his night because it meant she cared about him.

Jackson kissed her to shut her up. When her hands reached around his neck, he knew he'd been forgiven.

"There's something else you need to know, Mar. It's classified, but I have to tell you."

Her face became a serious mask. "What? You know you can tell me anything. Really, Jackson."

"I love you." Then he showed her exactly how he felt as his lips connected once again with hers. This time with all the longing and love he had felt for her these past two months. He hadn't lied about her being his reason to exist. She was his everything. His hands slid down her back, but he stopped when he tasted a tear.

She stared at him for a moment, a variety of emotions playing on her face, a single tear sliding down her cheek. Jackson worried that maybe he'd told her too soon.

"What's wrong, baby?" He moved back farther so he could get a better look at her.

Then she smiled. "I wasn't expecting that."

Jackson cocked an eyebrow at her odd response.

"I mean, it's great news, because I love you, too." Touching his cheek, she kissed him again. "I'd almost given up hope that we'd be able to see one another again, and I was so mad that I didn't tell you when we were on the plane," she whispered against his lips.

She loved him. Those words opened something in Jackson's heart and warmth spread through him.

He grinned. "So, how about that date. I bet we can catch a late meal and a midnight movie."

"We could." She pursed her delectable lips together. "But I was thinking we'd skip the movie and the dinner and go straight to dessert." Her left eyebrow rose and she gave him a wicked smile.

Then she shoved him back on the couch.

So much for the slow route.

"Are we playing the sheikh game again?" He waggled his eyebrows at her.

"No games, babe. This is you and me making one awesome dessert." She leaned over, pressing her breasts into his chest.

Jackson had a feeling he was never going to want for dessert the rest of his life. As she melded against him, his life felt as close to perfect as it ever could.

*Rancher Ramsey Westmoreland's temporary cook
is way too attractive for his liking.
Little does he know Chloe Burton came to his ranch
with another agenda entirely....*

That man across the street had to be, without a doubt, the most handsome man she'd ever seen.

Chloe Burton's pulse beat rhythmically as he stopped to talk to another man in front of a feed store. He was tall, dark and every inch of sexy—from his Stetson to the well-worn leather boots on his feet. And from the way his jeans and Western shirt fit his broad muscular shoulders, it was quite obvious he had everything it took to separate the men from the boys. The combination was enough to corrupt any woman's mind and had her weakening even from a distance. Her body felt flushed. It was hot. Unsettled.

Over the past year the only male who had gotten her time and attention had been the e-mail. That was simply pathetic, especially since now she was practically drooling simply at the sight of a man. Even his stance—both hands in his jeans pockets, legs braced apart, was a pose she would carry to her dreams.

And he was smiling, evidently enjoying the conversation being exchanged. He had dimples, incredibly sexy dimples in not one but both cheeks.

"What are you staring at, Clo?"

Chloe nearly jumped. She'd forgotten she had a lunch date. She glanced over the table at her best friend from college, Lucia Conyers.

"Take a look at that man across the street in the blue shirt, Lucia. Will he not be perfect for Denver's first issue of *Simply Irresistible* or what?" Chloe asked with so much excitement she almost couldn't stand it.

She was the owner of *Simply Irresistible*, a magazine for today's up-and-coming woman. Their once-a-year Irresistible Man cover, which highlighted a man the magazine felt deserved the honor, had increased sales enough for Chloe to open a Denver office.

When Lucia didn't say anything but kept staring, Chloe's smile widened. "Well?"

Lucia glanced across the booth at her. "Since you asked, I'll tell you what I see. One of the Westmorelands—Ramsey Westmoreland. And yes, he'd be perfect for the cover, but he won't do it."

Chloe raised a brow. "He'd get paid for his services, of course."

Lucia laughed and shook her head. "Getting paid won't be the issue, Clo—Ramsey is one of the wealthiest sheep ranchers in this part of Colorado. But everyone knows what a private person he is. Trust me—he won't do it."

Chloe couldn't help but smile. The man was the epitome of what she was looking for in a magazine cover and she was determined that whatever it took, he would be it.

"Umm, I don't like that look on your face, Chloe. I've seen it before and know exactly what it means."

She watched as Ramsey Westmoreland entered the store with a swagger that made her almost breathless. She *would* be seeing him again.

Look for Silhouette Desire's
HOT WESTMORELAND NIGHTS
by Brenda Jackson,
available March 9 wherever books are sold.

THE WESTMORELANDS

NEW YORK TIMES
bestselling author

BRENDA JACKSON

HOT WESTMORELAND NIGHTS

Ramsey Westmoreland knew better than to lust after the hired help. But Chloe, the new cook, was just so delectable. Though their affair was growing steamier, Chloe's motives became suspicious. And when he learned Chloe was carrying his child this Westmoreland Rancher had to choose between pride or duty.

Available March 2010 wherever books are sold.

Always Powerful, Passionate and Provocative.

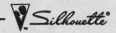

SPECIAL EDITION

FROM *USA TODAY* BESTSELLING AUTHOR
CHRISTINE RIMMER

A BRIDE FOR
JERICHO BRAVO

Marnie Jones had long ago buried her wild-child
impulses and opted to be "safe," romantically
speaking. But one look at born rebel Jericho Bravo
and she began to wonder if her thrill-seeking side
was about to be revived. Because if ever there was
a man worth taking a chance on, there he was,
right within her grasp....

*Available in March
wherever books are sold.*

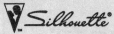

HARLEQUIN *Presents*

*Two families torn apart by secrets and desire
are about to be reunited in*

Hot Bed of Scandal

a sexy new duet by

Kelly Hunter

EXPOSED: MISBEHAVING WITH THE MAGNATE

#2905 Available March 2010

Gabriella Alexander returns to the French vineyard she
was banished from after being caught in flagrante with the
owner's son Lucien Duvalier—only to finish what they started!

REVEALED: A PRINCE AND A PREGNANCY

#2913 Available April 2010

Simone Duvalier wants Rafael Alexander and always has, but
they both get more than they bargained for when a night of
passion and a royal revelation rock their world!

REQUEST YOUR FREE BOOKS!

2 FREE NOVELS PLUS 2 FREE GIFTS!

HARLEQUIN®

Blaze™

Red-hot reads!

YES! Please send me 2 FREE Harlequin® Blaze™ novels and my 2 FREE gifts (gifts are worth about $10). After receiving them, if I don't wish to receive any more books, I can return the shipping statement marked "cancel." If I don't cancel, I will receive 6 brand-new novels every month and be billed just $4.24 per book in the U.S. or $4.71 per book in Canada. That's a saving of close to 15% off the cover price. It's quite a bargain. Shipping and handling is just 50¢ per book in the U.S. and 75¢ per book in Canada.* I understand that accepting the 2 free books and gifts places me under no obligation to buy anything. I can always return a shipment and cancel at any time. Even if I never buy another book, the two free books and gifts are mine to keep forever.

151 HDN E4CY   351 HDN E4CN

Name _____ (PLEASE PRINT) _____

Address _____ Apt. # _____

City _____ State/Prov. _____ Zip/Postal Code _____

Signature (if under 18, a parent or guardian must sign) _____

Mail to the Harlequin Reader Service:
IN U.S.A.: P.O. Box 1867, Buffalo, NY 14240-1867
IN CANADA: P.O. Box 609, Fort Erie, Ontario L2A 5X3

Not valid for current subscribers to Harlequin Blaze books.

Want to try two free books from another line?
Call 1-800-873-8635 or visit www.morefreebooks.com.

* Terms and prices subject to change without notice. Prices do not include applicable taxes. N.Y. residents add applicable sales tax. Canadian residents will be charged applicable provincial taxes and GST. Offer not valid in Quebec. This offer is limited to one order per household. All orders subject to approval. Credit or debit balances in a customer's account(s) may be offset by any other outstanding balance owed by or to the customer. Please allow 4 to 6 weeks for delivery. Offer available while quantities last.

Your Privacy: Harlequin Books is committed to protecting your privacy. Our Privacy Policy is available online at www.eHarlequin.com or upon request from the Reader Service. From time to time we make our lists of customers available to reputable third parties who may have a product or service of interest to you. If you would prefer we not share your name and address, please check here. ☐

Help us get it right—We strive for accurate, respectful and relevant communications. To clarify or modify your communication preferences, visit us at www.ReaderService.com/consumerchoice.

HB10

COMING NEXT MONTH

Available February 23, 2010

#525 BLAZING BEDTIME STORIES, VOLUME IV
Bedtime Stories
Kimberly Raye and Samantha Hunter

#526 TOO HOT TO HANDLE
Forbidden Fantasies
Nancy Warren

#527 HIS LITTLE BLACK BOOK
Encounters
Heather MacAllister

#528 LONE STAR LOVER
Stolen from Time
Debbi Rawlins

#529 POSSESSING MORGAN
Bonnie Edwards

#530 KNOWING THE SCORE
Marie Donovan

HBCNMBPA0210